— WESLEY ELLIS —

LONE STAR

AND THE
ALASKAN RENEGADES

JOVE BOOKS, NEW YORK

LONE STAR AND THE ALASKAN RENEGADES

A Jove Book / published by arrangement with
the author

PRINTING HISTORY
Jove edition / April 1991

ISBN: 0-515-10592-9

Jove Books are published by The Berkley Publishing Group,
200 Madison Avenue, New York, New York 10016.
The name "JOVE" and the "J" logo
are trademarks belonging to Jove Publications, Inc.

PRINTED IN THE UNITED STATES OF AMERICA

10 9 8 7 6 5 4 3 2 1

CREATURE OF DEATH!

Baker's eyes followed Jessie's pointing finger. His jaw dropped and then he gasped, "Oh my god! That's not a rock! That's a Greenland whale-shark, Miss Starbuck! It's damned near the size of a regular whale, and it's got a mouth and a set of teeth that'll bite through anything except chilled steel!"

"Do you know where its brain is?"

"Right at the end of its jaws, where its back starts to slant up. But you're not going to try to—"

Klaus came across the deck at a run, carrying Jessie's rifle. Stepping away from the two men, she levered a shell into the chamber and raised the rifle to her shoulder. . . .

LONE STAR

AND THE
ALASKAN RENEGADES

★

Chapter 1

"From the top of this rise we'll be within a half mile or so of the line fence, Ki," Jessie said as she reined in and looked at the gently upsloping ridge that rose ahead of them. "And we're not too far from the station stop."

"Are you suggesting that we ride on to the station and pick up the mail instead of sending Steve to get it?" Ki asked.

"That's what I have in mind," she nodded. "The idea just occurred to me that while we're so close to the depot we might as well swing by it and save having to send Steve or someone else all the way from the main house. It's still early, but the train's passed by now. And because of all the rain we've had, this is the first time Sun's been out of the paddock for almost a week."

"Then let's just angle up to the fence and follow it to the depot," Ki suggested. "Neither one of us has ridden a

1

line fence for such a long time that it'll come pretty close to being a new experience."

Jessie nudged Sun's flank with the toe of her boot. The magnificent palomino started moving again, tossing its head as though it understood that it was getting a reprieve from the small stable yard where it had been confined during the past four or five days. Ki followed Jessie's example and turned his own mount. They rode up the slope at a long slant, Jessie a short distance in the lead.

Even before Sun reached the top of the rise, Jessie could see the nearest posts and glistening top strands of the barbwire line fence that marked the Circle Star's northern boundary. As Sun continued his leisurely gait and more and more of the fence became visible, a frown formed on Jessie's face.

Turning in her saddle, she said to Ki, "Somebody went through that fence in a hurry and left their jacket dangling on it." She swiveled in her saddle to take a second look, and her voice took on an urgency it had not held before as she went on, "It's not just a jacket, Ki! That's a dead man hanging on the line fence!"

Ki's horse was now high enough on the slope to allow him to see the bottom strand of barbwire. He did not rein in when he reached Jessie's side, and she toed Sun ahead to keep abreast as they topped the hump of the rise.

What had seemed to be merely a bundle of clothing at Jessie's first glimpse was now completely visible and totally unmistakable. The corpse was suspended by its midsection on the bottom strand of barbwire, with only its back and shoulders visible. The dead man's head and arms dangled to the ground on the inner fence line while his legs were

2

stretched in an ungainly crisscrossed sprawl on the other side of the barbwire.

Ki was dismounting when Jessie reined in. He motioned her to stay back, but she ignored his gesture and stepped up beside him. Together they bent forward, and Ki reached out to turn the dead man's head and give them a clear view of his features for the first time.

"He's a total stranger to me, Ki," Jessie said. "I never saw him before. Did you?"

"No." Ki shook his head. He gestured to call Jessie's attention to the dead man's face, where several blotched bruises and lightly scabbed areas stood out against the death pallor that paled his tanned skin. Ki went on, "It's obvious that he was in a fight not too long before he died, a day or so perhaps. Long enough for his face to heal up pretty well."

"Yes," Jessie agreed. Then she put her finger on the frayed edges of the small hole centered in the dry, crusted brownish-red stain on the dead man's jacket and went on, "It's plain that he was shot before the rain started. If this bloodstain hadn't been dry and crusted, the rain would've caused it to spread more."

"Whoever killed him was a dead shot," Ki frowned. "One bullet."

"Yes," Jessie nodded. "And I'd say the killer fired that shot while this dead man was trying to get through the barbwire."

"And just left him hanging," Ki added. "He's probably been here for a day or two, maybe three or four."

"There's not much chance that we'll find any footprints or hoofprints, either," Jessie said thoughtfully. "On these

3

slopes the runoff from the rain would've wiped them out. There's no way of knowing how he got here or where he came from or which way he was traveling."

Ki nodded in agreement as he said, "It's pretty easy to see that the rain was lighter on this part of the range than it was around the main house where we were. In this high grass and with the ground as dry as it is here, any signs that might've told us which way he was traveling would be gone within a few hours."

"My guess is that he came from the railroad line." Jessie frowned. "It's only a mile or so away, and I'm sure you remember that the fence jogs a bit between here and the depot every place where it crosses a section line."

Ki nodded as he said, "You know, Jessie, we're really not far from the station, and we're heading in that direction anyhow. Let's ride on to it and see if Harry knows anything about this corpse. If he doesn't, we'll have him use the railroad telegraph and get his division superintendent to notify the sheriff."

"I was about to suggest the same thing." Jessie nodded. "It seems callous to ride away and leave that man's body hanging on the fence, but moving it might destroy some kind of evidence that Sheriff Connally would find useful when he gets here."

Ki said soberly, "The man's dead, Jessie. And from the position of his body it's pretty clear that he was shot before he got to the line fence. It's not our job to interfere in a case that doesn't involve the Circle Star."

"Of course it isn't," she agreed. After a moment of silence she went on, "You know, Ki, it could be that this dead man got these scrapes and bruises when he jumped off a moving train. The railroad tracks aren't very far from the line fence."

"Then who do you think shot him? There's no ranch house within three or four miles of these tracks."

"I don't have any ideas about that, Ki. And I don't intend to start guessing," Jessie replied. "I think this is a mystery that we'd better let Sheriff Connally try to solve. We have enough to do at the ranch, so let's just turn the problem over to him and spend our time taking care of our own affairs."

"I can't help but agree," Ki nodded. "Suppose we ride on to the station and get Harry to send that message we were talking about a few minutes ago."

Remounting, Jessie and Ki reined their mounts along the fence line and started for the whistle-stop.

"I'm sure glad to see you and Ki, Miss Jessie," Harry Walters, the station agent, greeted them as they entered the rough-walled little shanty that served as a depot for the whistle-stop. "But I didn't have time to let you know, being here by myself the way I am right now, with my helper gone."

"Let us know what?" Jessie asked. "And what's happened to your helper?"

"Oh, he had to go along and pump the handcar for Sheriff Connally, seeing as how the sheriff couldn't pump it hisself on account of his wound," Walters replied. "But he said he'd be coming right on back—the sheriff, that is—soon as the doc gets him fixed up."

"Sheriff Connally's hurt?" Ki asked. "How?"

"Why, it seems like he was on the eastbound passenger haul, bringing back a prisoner that he'd gone to pick up at some little place along the line west. Just a little while after the train they was on passed the station here, the prisoner

5

winged the sheriff with a snub-nosed derringer he'd had hid away."

"What happened then?" As Jessie asked the question a puzzled frown was forming on her brow. She went on, "Was there a gunfight? I can't imagine the sheriff backing away, when all the prisoner had was a derringer."

"Maybe one shot was all he had, but he sure done his best to put the sheriff to rest," Walters replied. "That one slug put Sheriff Connally's right arm plumb outa business. He couldn't get his Colt outa the holster in time to drop the prisoner before he'd managed to jump off of the train."

"But in spite of being wounded, Sheriff Connally followed the man who was escaping and shot him?" Ki asked.

"He didn't talk about it much, but I'd say that things got pretty lively for a while," Walters said.

"I've always considered Sheriff Connally to be a very careful man," Jessie said. "I just can't imagine him letting a prisoner escape or overlooking a gun when he was searching for one."

"Seems like this fellow had his derringer hid in his boot," Walters went on. "Anyways, after he'd shot the sheriff, the jailbird yanked the jump line—that's the brake-valve cord that stops the train right away, in case you don't follow railroad talk, Miss Jessie. Now, when a train gets stopped thataways it bucks the whole string like a fresh bronco for a minute or two, and while it was still bucking and jarring, the prisoner jumped outa the coach and begun running, with the sheriff hotfooting it after him."

Walters stopped for breath, and Jessie took the opportunity to turn to Ki and say, "That was the prisoner's body we passed on the way here."

"If you passed a dead man, it was bound to be him,"

Walters broke in before Ki could reply. "Sheriff Connally said he was bleeding pretty good from that derringer slug, and he didn't have enough strength with just one good arm to carry the body back to the train, so he just left the dead man hanging on the line fence. Then he had the engineer back the train up here, it being the closest place he could think of to get a bandage on his arm. Well, now, the first minute I seen the sheriff, it was plain as day that what he needed was a doctor. Soon as I done the best I could to stanch his bleeding, I told the swampie to get him back on that train and head for town."

"I guess he won't be coming back for a while, then," Ki remarked to Jessie. "We'd better—"

Before he could finish, Walters broke in and said, "If you got business with the sheriff, he oughta be getting here right soon. He allowed as how he'd best get that dead man's body off of the fence and wind up the case."

"We don't have any reason to wait," Jessie replied. "But you might tell him that if he needs any help from the Circle Star, he'll certainly get it. Ki and I were riding the line fence when we saw the dead man, and we decided to come on here and find out if you knew anything about what had happened and to pick up our mail at the same time. If you've got the pouch handy, we'll just take it and go on our way."

"I'll have to get it out for you, Miss Starbuck," Walters said. "Like I always do, I put it in the safe."

Turning to the massive safe that stood in one corner of the crowded little station, he opened it and took out the large leather pouch that bore the familiar Circle Star brand on its flap. He was handing it to Jessie when the distant whistle of a locomotive sounded outside.

"That'll be the accommodation the sheriff said he was going

7

to ask the district super for," Walters told them. "It'll be here in just a minute or two, and you can see for yourself how the sheriff's getting on, if you feel like you can put off leaving."

Turning to Ki, Jessie said, "We're certainly not in that big a hurry. Let's wait."

"Of course." Ki nodded. "I'm as curious as you are."

They stepped out onto the platform that bridged the gap between the building and the rails. The accommodation train was just coming around the last curve and was already slowing for its stop as it entered the side track that ran from the main line to the building. It was a short string, a locomotive and tender, a boxcar and a passenger coach. As the little two-car drag stopped with the passenger coach in front of the platform with a final squeal of brakes, Sheriff Connally appeared on the bottom step of the passenger car's vestibule.

"Well, Miss Starbuck," he said, "It's not often that I find such a charming lady waiting for me. I'm flattered."

Jessie looked up from her inspection of the sling that cradled Connally's right arm to say, "We're all just glad to see that you're not hurt as badly as you might've been."

"It wasn't much of a fracas," he replied. "I'm right glad to see you and Ki here, because it solves a problem I've been puzzling over since we pulled out of the depot back in town."

"What sort of problem could you possibly have with the Circle Star?" She frowned. "That outlaw didn't even get across the line fence onto our range."

"Oh, I wasn't thinking about the body of that fellow hanging on your line fence, Miss Starbuck." The sheriff was stepping off the coach onto the station platform as he spoke.

He went on, "I was trying to figure out how to get your guest to the Circle Star's main house without having to ride with him all the way."

"Guest?" Jessie frowned. "I haven't invited any visitors to the ranch lately, Sheriff. And you know that when we're expecting guests either one of the hands or Ki or I will meet them with the buckboard to carry their luggage."

A voice that was strange to Jessie, the voice of a man, spoke from the shadowed vestibule. "You are Miss Starbuck, then? And you did not my message receive?"

Both Jessie and the sheriff peered into the vestibule. The man who'd spoken was now moving down to its bottom step. He was leaning forward, his head tilted downward, his features hidden by his stance as well as by the sharp shadow-line that dimmed the coach's entrance. Then Sheriff Connally stepped out to the platform, and the speaker behind him moved to the bottom step and stood blinking at the bright sunshine.

One quick glance was enough for Jessie to recognize that his black, closely fitting four-button serge coat had been tailored in Europe, and she shifted the focus of her gaze to the stranger's face. He was leaning forward, and though the brim of his low-crowned derby hat shaded most of his face, she could see his lips and square jaw and the tip of his blunt nose. She guessed the newcomer's age to be in the early thirties. At the same time her mind was busy placing the phrasing of his question as fitting into the Germanic style of speech.

He went on, "I have a great distance traveled to meet with you, Miss Starbuck. Please permit that I introduce myself." The newcomer's speech was almost completely unaccented, but carefully articulated and structured, a sure sign that

English was not his native tongue. He was straightening his back as he spoke, now he bowed from the waist as he went on, "I am Klaus Reiden, of *Das Kapital Privatbank*, in Berlin."

"Of course!" Jessie exclaimed as she extended her hand. "We've exchanged letters a number of times, but haven't had the pleasure of meeting in person until now."

"It is to my great regret that in becoming acquainted personally we have been so long delayed," Reiden said as he took Jessie's hand and bowed over it. "To visit your country and the great ranch you own I have for many years wished, but this is my first opportunity. However, I cannot understand your surprise at my arrival. I have written you that I would be here."

"Now that you're here, you're certainly welcome," Jessie assured him. "And your letter's probably in that mail pouch Ki's holding." Gesturing as she went on, "Ki is— Well, in your country, I suppose he'd be called my confidential assistant."

"Ki?" Reiden's facial expression did not change, but a frown was in the tone of his voice as he extended his hand to Ki. When they'd clasped hands for a moment and exchanged nods, he turned back to Jessie and went on, "My curiosity you must forgive, but is an Oriental assistant not strange here in your country?"

Jessie answered before Ki could speak. "Nothing's strange to us in America," she smiled. "Especially here in the West."

Before she and young Reiden could continue their conversation, Sheriff Connally broke in to say, "I don't aim to be butting in, Miss Jessie, but I'm sorta working on borrowed time. I need to wind up my business here and get back

10

to town before the next train is due on the main line."

"Of course!" Jessie replied. "We're standing here chatting and keeping you from getting on with your work."

"If there's anything I can do to help you . . . " Ki began as he turned to Connally.

Shaking his head, the sheriff said, "Not a thing, Ki, but thanks all the same. I just come here to do one job, get that outlaw's body that I left dangling on the Circle Star's line fence. I'd've toted him into town with me, but the train had to move on, and I was by myself on foot. I wasn't able to lift him off of the barbwire on account of that slug he'd put in my arm."

"Yes. We passed him on the way here," Jessie nodded. "Of course, we didn't know then that you'd shot him, so we rode on here to the station to report finding him."

Walters broke in to say, "I told Miss Starbuck what had happened, Sheriff. Or at least as much as I knowed about it."

"Good," Connally nodded. "Now, if you'll pass the word to the engineer, we'll get back on the main line and finish our job while the track's still clear."

When the sheriff and Walters began talking Jessie had returned her attention to Reiden. She told him, "We keep three or four of the ranch horses here in the station's corral, so we can provide a mount for you to ride with us to the main house. You do know how to handle a horse, I'm sure."

Nodding, he replied, "The riding academy I have attended, Miss Starbuck, but with your western broncos I am not familiar. I hope it is not one of the wild unbroken ones such as I have read about in the books of Karl May."

"These are just saddle horses, not broncos, so you shouldn't have any trouble." She smiled. "But if you have

11

any bulky luggage, we'll have to send one of the Circle Star hands after it in the buckboard tomorrow."

"Besides my bag, here, I have a small steamer trunk in the baggage car," he replied. "But I have tried to put all that I will need at once into my portmanteau."

"Your trunk can wait, then," Jessie nodded. Addressing Walters once more, she went on, "I'm sure you'll take care of getting it off the train?"

"Of course, Miss Jessie," he assured her. "I'll have it ready and waiting. And talking about waiting, I better go see what the sheriff needs for me to do now."

As Walters turned away from them, young Reiden turned to Jessie and said, "I have heard so much about your famous ranch that I am anxious to see it for myself. I must admit that I have had difficulty in imagining what it must be like. I understand that it is as large as some of the small nations close to my homeland."

"People generally exaggerate size." Jessie smiled. "There are other ranches in Texas as large as the Circle Star, and some that are even bigger. But I gather that you've come to America on a business trip?"

"That is correct," he nodded. "And the most important business I have is with you, Miss Starbuck."

"I can't think what it would be." Jessie frowned. "I don't recall any problems with the few ventures we have in Europe."

"Please understand, Miss Starbuck, I am not trying to be mysterious or forcing you to guess," Reiden said earnestly. "But I am not accustomed to the great distances I have been traveling. If you will indulge me, it will be much easier for us to discuss business after you have read the letter you have said must be in your mail pouch."

"Of course I will," she agreed. "I get travel-tired myself at times. We'll postpone our business discussions until we're at the Circle Star, after I've read your letter and we've finished supper."

★

Chapter 2

"I must confess, Miss Starbuck, that I am somewhat over-come by the size of your Circle Star Ranch," Klaus Reiden observed. He was sitting with Jessie and Ki in the room that had been her father's study. "From what I saw and from some of the things you and Ki told me during our long ride from the railway station, your ranch is as large as some of the smaller provinces in my homeland."

"That's due to my father's vision," Jessie said quickly. "I can't take any credit for the Circle Star's size. But I'd have a great deal of difficulty without Ki to attend to a lot of the details of running it."

"Now, Jessie, you know better than that," Ki put in. "I never had seen a really big American ranch and didn't know anything about cattle until Alex set up the Circle Star and began to stock the range."

"You are both too modest," Reiden smiled. "Through

Alex Starbuck's dealings with my father I've learned a bit about your other holdings, and I wonder how you find the time to oversee such a vast and busy enterprise as this ranch and still stay in touch with all the other interests you have."

"With a lot of help from Ki, I manage somehow to keep up with everything," Jessie replied. "And speaking of other interests, the letter you sent telling me when you'd arrive and mentioning the reason for your visit was in the mailbag, just as I'd expected."

"And have you had the time to read it?"

"To read it, but not to study it," she told Reiden. "I just scanned through it to get the main points."

"And I hope your look was enough to allow you to form an opinion of the offer I have come here to make?"

Jessie shook her head as she said, "I didn't have time to think through everything it touched. And I'm a little bit reluctant to form any sort of opinion until I've gone through Alex's files and found out the details of his purchase of the land you're offering to buy."

"You must know the material in your father's files is much the same as that in ours," Reiden persisted. "This is not the first offer we have made for the Alaskan coal deposits in which we are interested."

"Oh, I understand that, of course. I don't question the points you made in your letter, and I'm sure you'll make a fair offer for the land you want to buy. But I'm equally sure you'll understand why I must take a bit of time deciding whether or not I want to sell any of my properties."

Reiden nodded and went on, "I do not wish to press you into a quick decision, Miss Starbuck. And I have no doubt that I'll enjoy spending today in the field with your men, for

I have thought for a great deal of time about the many things I should like to learn about your American West. We will wait, then, until the evening to discuss our business."

"I'm glad we finally found these papers," Jessie told Ki as they entered the big room that was the center of their activity when they were at the Circle Star.

She and Ki had just waved good-bye to Klaus Reiden as he rode off with a group of the ranch hands to spend the day riding the line fences. As Jessie spoke she gestured toward the green enameled metal lockbox that stood on the desk at one side of the room.

Jessie went on, "It's been such a long time since we went to look at the Alaskan properties that I'm not sure I'd recall all the details of those coal deposits today."

"I can understand that," Ki replied. "And I know as little about them as you do. There's never been any need to worry about them, so we've just left everything alone."

"I haven't really looked at them," she said as she stepped up to the table where the lockbox rested. "I just took time to open the box and make sure it's the one that holds the few records Alex left of his trips to Alaska."

"We'll have plenty of time to go through the box and find the papers we need," Ki said. He was moving up to join Jessie as she opened the dust-covered storage file.

"Speaking of papers," Jessie went on. She'd unlocked the box after brushing away the film of fine dust that had gathered on it. "Did you have time this morning to look at the newspapers that were in the mailbag and check the prices that range-finished steers are bringing now at the Fort Worth Livestock Exchange?"

"No, but they can't be much higher than they were last

week," Ki replied. He was taking the file jackets as Jessie removed them from the box and spreading them on the tabletop. He added, "Of course, by now the buyers might have a better idea how the cattle market's going to be affected by the drought that struck the southeast Texas range this spring."

"From everything I can gather, it was really a bad one," Jessie replied. She spoke without looking up from the file jackets they were now examining. "And you know how lucky we were here on the Circle Star. We got most of the rain that usually just passes us by in the clouds blowing east."

"I've certainly noticed the same thing you have," Ki went on. "That with the roundup coming on, we'll have a very heavy herd to ship, much heavier than last year's."

"If we're still here when it's time for the roundup," Jessie said as she looked up from the sheaf of papers she'd been thumbing through.

"I've never heard you say that before," Ki told her. A frown was forming on his usually inscrutable face as he went on, "I can't remember how long it's been since we missed a roundup."

"Quite a few years," she replied thoughtfully. "But here's the file we've been looking for. Let's put off talking about the roundup and see how we feel after we've found out what sort of problem young Klaus Reiden has brought us from Germany."

"You sound very serious, Jessie," Ki observed. "There can't be anything earthshaking about what the Reiden bank is proposing, but it must be important or they wouldn't have sent a member of the family such a distance to talk with you about it."

18

"I had our privacy in mind when I suggested that young Reiden might enjoy going out for the day with the range hands," she told Ki. "I'm sure that if he stayed here with us he'd have wanted to join us while we were studying the proposal he sent."

"Yes. I caught on to that from the beginning." Ki nodded. "Since he showed up so unexpectedly at the whistle-stop we've had so little time to talk privately that I don't yet know exactly what's in this proposal the European financiers are making."

"I've only had time to glance at it myself," Jessie said. "But as briefly as possible, they're offering to buy an immense tract of land that Alex owned. He'd hit a rich gold strike, but the cost of developing it was more than he could afford at the time. Just how he happened to be in a position to borrow money from the Reiden bank while he was prospecting in Alaska is something I haven't found out yet."

"Gold!" Ki exclaimed. His usually level voice rose in surprise when he spoke the single word. Jessie nodded without speaking, and Ki went on, his perplexity reflected in the tone of his voice, "I don't really know a great deal about your father's Alaskan days, Jessie. Remember, when I joined Alex he had already settled his headquarters in San Francisco."

Nodding, Jessie went on, "And I don't know much more than you would about what he did in Alaska. He talked very little about his experiences there. It was as though he wanted to draw a curtain or close a door on them."

"That was the feeling I got, too," Ki agreed. "Even when I first met him. He hadn't been able to get passage on a ship to California, so he took a Japanese freighter that was returning to its home port, because he knew that he could easily get to America from Japan. I remember it well, for that was when he ran into me in Fusan."

Ki had no need to elaborate on his reference to the obscure Japanese port. He knew that Jessie was familiar with the details of his chance encounter with her father, and also knew that she was well aware of the chasm that had opened between his mother and his mother's family after her runaway marriage to a young American naval officer, who in his early youth had been a close friend of Alex Starbuck.

While Ki's grandfather was acting as liaison officer for the United States Consulate in Japan, his mother had met and fallen in love with the young American naval officer who would be Ki's father. His mother's parents refused to give permission for their daughter to marry the foreigner, and Ki's parents eloped. Their marriage opened a chasm between daughter and parents, but only tightened their bond to one another.

When his parents were lost during a storm at sea, and Ki found neither consolation nor shelter in the home of his grandparents, he set out to make his own life. Even at the early age of his abandonment by his mother's family, Ki had acquired skill in the art of unarmed combat. Having no other recourse, he became a traveling mercenary, a warrior-for-hire, moving from one martial *do* to another in hand-to-mouth survival.

Coincidence had brought him into contact with Alex Starbuck, who at that time was a regular visitor to the Orient in search of merchandise for the small shop he'd opened on the San Francisco waterfront. On learning that Ki was the son of his childhood chum, Alex offered Ki a job as his man-of-all-work. From that time on, Ki served Alex faithfully. Following Alex's untimely and brutal death at the hands of killers sent by the sinister European cabal that he'd been fighting, Ki transferred his allegiance to Jessie.

Caught up in memories of the past, Ki went on, "As you well know, Jessie, I joined your father when I was very young, but even then he'd put his Alaskan days behind him. Remember, when we first met, Alex was returning to America from what turned out to be his last visit to Alaska. On our voyage to this country he talked a great deal about my father and mother, of course. But he said very little about his Alaskan days."

Both Jessie and Ki fell silent as their minds were drawn into memories of a time they had been left behind. To Jessie, her father had been a kindly but somewhat distant man whom she'd rarely seen but adored from afar. Not only was Alex busy in the process of earning the huge fortune, which she inherited, but he was still mourning his beloved wife, who'd died giving birth to Jessie.

When Alex Starbuck grew tired of roving, he supported himself by opening a small shop on the San Francisco waterfront. His stock in trade at that time was the array of curios and art objects that he'd bought during his travels in the Far East. From this very modest beginning he'd created such a sizeable business that regular trips to the Orient became necessary to replace his stock.

Alex's industry combined with the financial acumen he'd acquired soon brought prosperity, and by his shrewd judgment in making profitable investments, his prosperity became wealth. From his modest start in the little curio store on the San Francisco waterfront he expanded his business interests until he could be classified as one of the multimillionaire moguls of an expanding America. Even before his marriage he'd become a millionaire many times over. Ki became Alex's good right hand, his loyal helper as well as his friend.

Not all of Alex's life was rosy, however. Through his financial contacts in Europe he'd learned about the existence of a cartel that had been formed by a greedy coalition of wealthy European financiers to acquire the control of America's wealth by fair means or foul. Unable to awaken eastern politicians, who dominated Washington, to the danger of the cartel, and driven by his patriotism, Alex counterattacked the cartel, using his knowledge and skill and spending freely of his huge fortune to thwart its sinister plans.

To create a safe haven where he could find shelter from time to time, Alex bought the thousands of acres of grazing range in Texas that he consolidated into the Circle Star. He also counted on it being a home for himself and Jessie, and in the false security of the vast spread of open range, his vigilance relaxed. It was on the Circle Star that the hired gunmen of the cartel ended Alex's life with a burst of gunfire during a surprise attack.

Jessie was in her last year at an exclusive woman's college in the East when Alex was murdered. By that time she'd grown to be mature enough to handle the shock of his assassination, and to take on the responsibilities that her father's will passed on to her. Without hesitation, Ki transferred to her the loyalty that he'd given to Alex.

It was with his help that Jessie gradually took firm control of the extensive Starbuck holdings. During the relatively short span of years devoted to expanding his business holdings Alex had built a financial empire.

Although his wealth had been based on the solid foundation of gold, silver and copper mines scattered throughout the mountain West, to his mining interests he'd added timber operations along both the California coast and the Canadian border. In the new raw towns that were built near his mining and timber holdings he'd established banks, and soon his growing wealth and diversified interests had made it necessary for him to seek a seat on the stock exchange, which brought him into contact with men even wealthier than he was.

Until the death of his beloved wife in giving birth to Jessie, Alex had made San Francisco his seat of operations. Then the continued danger from the sinister European cartel seeking to master America's industrial riches led him to form the vast Circle Star Ranch in Texas.

Taking up the battle with the cartel, Jessie and Ki fought its minions for several years until its masters were eliminated. The cartel dissolved, riven by internal friction over a choice of new leadership and the relentless pursuit of its members by Jessie and Ki. Freed from the cartel's machinations at last, Jessie and Ki then continued to work together to preserve and even to expand the vast industrial and commercial empire that Alex Starbuck had created.

Now, sitting with Ki in the room that had been Alex Starbuck's study, holding an envelope that contained documents tied to Alex's early days, Jessie studied the envelope for a moment, as though merely by gazing at its age-browned surface she could fathom the secret it held inside. Shaking her head to bring herself back into the present, she ripped the flap open and took out the thin sheaf of folded sheets of paper it contained.

23

She scanned the pages quickly, flipping them over one after the other until she reached the last page. Then she looked up at Ki, a small frown forming on her face.

"Most of these papers are survey notes and descriptions," she told him. "They document the mining claims that Alex filed in Alaska. The envelope's just labeled 'Alaska,' but of course I haven't any idea where they might be. There's one thing that baffles me completely, though."

"Oh? What is it?"

"This one sheet of paper in a separate envelope. Ki, do you want to look at all this yourself, in case I might've missed something?"

"From what I've seen during the past few minutes there's never been a chance that you've overlooked a single thing," Ki smiled. "Suppose you just tell me about the page that you're finding so puzzling."

"If it means anything at all, it must mean that Alex made a rather strange agreement with Klaus Reiden's father." She frowned. "But I think I understand why it was made, even if I did have to do a bit of reading between the lines."

"Go ahead, then," Ki suggested. "Tell me what it's all about."

"Alex must've been pretty hard-pressed for ready cash at the time he wrote and signed this," Jessie went on. "It's a note acknowledging a loan from Klaus Reiden's father, and agreeing to repay it with reasonable interest on demand."

"It's probably a copy of the original note," Ki said. "We both know that Alex was forced to borrow money quite often during the years when he was just beginning to branch out from his curio shop."

"I've seen a lot of promissory notes and other kinds of documents since I became responsible for everything I inherited from Alex, but I've never seen a promissory note like this before, Ki," Jessie went on. "It doesn't give any figures at all. It's just a blank IOU acknowledging a loan from Klaus Reiden's father. Here, look at it for yourself."

"I'll have to agree that it's unusual, not at all like Alex," Ki said thoughtfully after he'd studied the brief inscription for a moment. "Though I suppose there's a reason why the note doesn't specify a definite amount; Alex had his own way of doing things. He never tried to make a secret of being hard-pressed for money a lot of the time he was in Alaska."

"But there's absolutely nothing at all specified in this," Jessie said. "Not the amount Alex borrowed or the interest he'd be paying, or even the dates when the note was signed and when payment is due. And it doesn't mention whether or not the lender can follow the usual banking practice of compounding the interest and adding it to the amount that's overdue."

A frown was forming on Ki's face as he went on. "That's just not the way Alex did business, Jessie, you know that. Whether he was borrowing or lending, he was always a stickler for details of that sort."

"But this is Alex's signature on the note," Jessie went on. "You know quite well that neither of us could be mistaken about it, Ki. A forgery's the first thing we'd have noticed. Besides that, all the papers of his that we have here at the Circle Star were brought here by you or me or by Alex himself."

"That's true," Ki agreed. "And during all the years I spent with Alex, I never knew him to be anything but meticulously precise in any paperwork." While he was speaking Ki was examining the note a second time, holding it up to the

25

light coming through an open window. He turned back to Jessie and nodded.

"I'm sure it's authentic," he agreed. "And I'm equally sure that there was never a time during all the years I spent with Alex when I saw this envelope or any of these papers."

"And not only did Alex deal with the Reiden family bank for many years, he and Klaus's father became close friends," Jessie said thoughtfully. She was silent for a moment, then went on, "I've been trying to think of any reason why Alex would sign a note of this sort, Ki."

"And so have I," Ki nodded. "I'm sure you know that, though. I'm as baffled as you are, Jessie. The only reason I can think of that would've caused Alex to put his name on a note of this sort—or even to have written it—is that it was some sort of private joke between him and Klaus Reiden's father."

Jessie shook her head, and her voice was firm when she replied, "No, Ki. Alex wasn't the sort of man who joked about money. And though I only met Gustaf Reiden once, when he was visiting Alex during my late childhood, he didn't strike me as the sort of man who'd joke about money, either. The best thing we can do is to wait until Klaus gets back and hope that he'll have some sort of answer to our puzzle."

Chapter 3

"For coming so late to breakfast, I must to you and Ki apologize, Miss Starbuck," Klaus Reiden said as he hurried into the study.

Jessie and Ki were sitting on the divan. Jessie smiled as she replied, "No apologies are called for. And please don't be so formal; we're not used to it here in Texas. Everyone just calls me Jessie."

"Very well, it shall be Jessie, then," he nodded. "And to you and Ki, I am now Klaus."

"Good," Jessie nodded. "Now, I have a hunch that after your experiences yesterday you'll be glad to have a bit of extra rest. Anybody does who isn't accustomed to spending a day on horseback on the Texas range."

"This is true." Klaus nodded. He was more at ease now; the Germanic phrasing that had been so noticeable when he first entered the room had vanished from his speech. He went on, "And in the homeland, horses are few. Today our country has only three companies of mounted soldiers, and the few remaining horses belong to the aristocrats and the large farm-owners."

"I suppose that while you were out on the range with them yesterday, the hands gave you the usual lessons they reserve for a tenderfoot?" Ki asked.

"My day with them was what you would call an experience," he replied. "But I can now remain for a while in the saddle on the back of what they called a bronco. And almost I can a lasso throw. But I cannot yet stay on a horse that is running wildly and rope a cow at the same time, as they do so easily. And the salted coffee I cannot yet enjoy when I drink."

"That was your introduction to the Texas range," Ki told him. "But you've passed it now. If it makes you feel any better, the hands on every ranch hereabouts give the same treatment to every tenderfoot who shows up."

"But I am not accustomed yet to riding a great distance in the early morning and then learning to do what you call throwing a loop," Klaus said. "I am afraid I have slept over."

"That's not important," Jessie assured him. "Ki and I had a biscuit and some coffee, and by now the cook's had time to clear away after the hands have eaten. He's probably ready to serve our regular breakfast, so suppose we go over there. We can talk while we're eating."

"That's good," Klaus told her. "For I am very hungry indeed."

"Ranch life does have that effect on anybody who isn't used to it," Jessie said as she stood up. "After breakfast we'll come back here where we can talk privately."

"While you were out on the range yesterday, Ki and I went over Alex's old files," Jessie told Klaus Reiden after they'd settled down in the study following breakfast.

"And did you find the papers you were seeking?" Reiden asked.

"Yes, of course. There were plat maps and survey notes of the Alaskan property you're interested in," she replied. "We haven't looked at them closely yet, though we also found something that I'm wondering about, an item that might be duplicated in the papers you brought with you from Germany."

"I am sure I know to what you refer," Reiden said quickly. "It could only have been a copy of the promissory note which your father gave to mine."

"I was positive you'd know what it was when I mentioned it," Jessie nodded. "And I'm equally positive that you must have a legal copy of it, one that gives the date on which it fell due and a definite figure of the amount it covers."

Young Reiden was silent for a long moment, then he said slowly, "The copy which you found is a precise duplicate of the one which my father from yours received. The note is for any amount my father chooses to request."

"For any amount!" Jessie exclaimed. "Oh, no! Alex would never have signed a note of that kind unless he intended it to be just a joke! Why, whoever holds it could demand everything that my father owned when he died!"

"You must realize that we would never make any sort of outrageous or unjust demand," Klaus said calmly. "But with all respect, Jessie, your father's signature on the promissory note is quite legal. My father a letter has from your father which refers to the note as being valid."

"I'm not worrying about you and your father, Klaus. I'm well aware of your family's reputation for honesty and fairness. But suppose—well, suppose your father's copy somehow got into the hands of some unscrupulous individual who might make some sort of outrageous claim?"

"We have taken all the precautions possible to safeguard our files, Jessie. The document for which you have so much concern is in my father's private safe," young Reiden replied. "Such a thing could not possibly happen."

"Just the same, I'd like for you to let me draft a new note that didn't have the sky for a limit and trade it for the one you now have," Jessie went on.

"If the decision was mine to make, I would be more than pleased to oblige you, Jessie," Klaus said. "But the instructions from my father I do not dare disobey."

Jessie recognized in Klaus's reply the stubborn strain common to the Germanic clans. Realizing her disadvantage, she played for time. She said, "Until now, we've just barely mentioned coal as being the reason why you took the time and trouble to come here, Klaus. Is there something else you're after?"

Klaus shook his head. "There is nothing more. The only reason my father has sent me here is to get a clear title to the great deposits of coal that lie under your father's Alaskan claim. In all honesty, Jessie, I must tell you that right at this time coal is more precious to our people than gold, and in the future the value of the Alaskan coal veins can only increase."

"But Alaska's so far from Germany, Klaus!" Jessie protested. "And I've always thought there was plenty of coal in Europe."

"Until now there has been." Klaus nodded. "But the veins

in our Saar provinces will not last forever. Other countries have as little coal left as we do; some have already reached the end of their deposits."

"But is it practical to ship coal all the way from Alaska to Germany?" Jessie frowned.

"Very much so," Klaus nodded. "With the shipping, we have no worry. By sailing during the summer months through the polar seas a vessel from Alaska can reach German ports in less time than a ship from Europe can sail across the Atlantic Ocean to reach the eastern coast of your country."

Jessie was silent for a moment, then she said, "You and your father have been giving a great deal of thought to this, haven't you?"

"I have had little to do with it; all the credit goes to my father," Klaus replied. "I am only carrying out the instructions he has to me given."

Jessie's silence this time lasted even longer than before. At last she said, "Suppose you tell me just what sort of deal it is that you're proposing."

"A very simple one," Klaus replied. "All that my family wishes are the coal veins to mine. For this we are offering to buy the land under which the coal deposits are to be found."

"That sounds like a straightforward offer," Jessie said. "But suppose that while you're mining the coal you run into a vein of gold?"

"In exchange for the coal you will receive a quit-claim to all the minerals that remain, whether they are gold or other metals."

"Your family is anxious to start mining at once, then?" Ki asked.

"Perhaps not at once." Klaus frowned. "But at the time

when the coal is most needed by the factories of our country. How far in the future that will be we cannot now know."

"Your offer sounds very fair to me," Jessie said. "And I'm sure that we can agree, but I'd like a little more time to go over the other papers that were in Alex's old file."

"I would certainly not object to that." Klaus nodded. "Do you think it will a great deal of time require?"

"Very little, I'd say," Jessie replied. "But Ki and I had very little time to examine them, and I'd like to be sure there weren't some sort of notes or agreements that might change my mind about the deal we're discussing."

"Then by all means, examine the papers." Klaus nodded. "I will welcome the time for which it will free me to look more at this amazing ranch of yours. I am sure that you can spare one of your many cowboys to go with me and keep me from getting lost in its vastness."

Neither Jessie nor Ki replied to Klaus for a moment; they had turned their heads to glance at each other in the silent communication that had developed during the years of their shared dangers. Jessie nodded first, then Ki smiled and inclined his head a fraction of an inch. Jessie turned back to Klaus.

"Perhaps you'd enjoy your day more if I rode with you," she suggested. "We've had several days of rain, and I haven't spent as much time outdoors as I like to."

"This I would enjoy very much," Klaus agreed. "On the long train ride I have just finished, I could do nothing except sit and look through the window at the passing landscape."

"Yes, I know the feeling," Jessie nodded. "After several days on a train, I'm ready to get to a place where I can feel fresh air in my face and go where I want to instead of where railroad track forces me to."

"That is what I noticed on the long trip here," Klaus told her. "And I saw many places which I should have liked to go to a closer look to get."

"Then suppose we just push business into the background for the rest of the day? We'll have plenty of time to devote to it after supper."

"This is a sensible thing you propose, Jessie," Klaus agreed. "And it is pleasant as well for me to have you show me yourself more of this great ranch. As for the transaction which has brought me here, I am sure that we will have no problems an agreement reaching."

"It's a beautiful day," Jessie said to Klaus Reiden as the Circle Star's main building dropped out of sight. They'd been riding a gentle upslope for a half hour or more; now they had topped its low crest line and were dropping behind one of the long ridges that here and there broke the sameness of the broad, rolling range. Its growth of thick high grass extended as far ahead as they could see.

"Yes," Klaus agreed. "And though I know a great deal less about horses than you do, it is easy to see that yours is enjoying the fine weather as much as we are."

As usual, Jessie was riding Sun. After having had a day of rest the big palomino was showing his readiness for another long ride on the ranch's broad stretches. Now and then he would toss his head and start to prance as a preliminary move toward going into a gallop, forcing Jessie to keep a careful hand on his reins.

"Oh, Sun always acts this way for a little while, especially right after he's gotten out on open range," Jessie told him. "He'd like to be out here every day instead of having to spend so much of his time in the corral."

"I think such a fine animal I have never before seen," Klaus went on.

"Since Sun can't thank you for the compliment, Klaus, I will," Jessie said. Then she commented, "I've noticed that you seem at home on horseback. Do you have a chance to ride much at home, in Germany?"

"Not as much as I should like," he replied. "Such open country as this we are riding over now, we do not have. There were times yesterday when I felt envy for the sort of life led by your—is it not cowhands you call them?"

"I've heard them called by a lot of names." Jessie smiled. "Not only cowhands, but cowboys, wranglers, buckaroos, cowpokes, saddle stiffs, ranahans, waddies, cowpunchers, vaqueros, bronc twisters—those are just a few of the more pleasant ones."

"Whatever your men are called, all of them ride well," Klaus said. "I will admit that after watching them I should have liked to gallop on my horse a bit, but they were too solicitous of my safety, or did not trust my riding skill. But that perhaps was because I did not bring my boots and other riding wear from home with me."

"It's not the boots and breeches that make a rider," Jessie smiled. "Though I'd've been glad to lend you riding gear if what I had would fit you. But riding with you today, I can see that you don't have anything to apologize for."

"I enjoy it here even more than at home, where we do not have such great expanses of open country," he went on. "It is here on your American prairie that I at last am coming to realize that horsemanship is not an empty exercise, but a need."

"If you still have an urge to gallop, we can give our horses their head right now," she suggested. "There's plenty of

34

open range in all directions, and Sun would welcome a little bit of a workout. As for that, so would I."

"Then by all means let us for a short distance gallop."

As he spoke, Klaus dug his heels into his mount's flanks and the feisty cow pony broke into a gallop. Jessie had not expected Klaus to respond so quickly and was a few moments behind him in spurring Sun to the faster gait.

She saw Klaus twist his head to look back, then he drummed his heels on his mount's barrel. His horse was already moving faster than Sun. Jessie knew that if she let the palomino have free rein it could easily close the gap between them and pass Klaus, but she decided to give her guest the gratification of holding the lead he'd already gained.

With only a minimum amount of occasional pressure on Sun's reins to be sure of maintaining the gap between them, she followed Klaus's galloping mount in its course across the rolling prairie with the breeze brushing their faces. A long curving upslope rose ahead of them. Instead of turning his horse to one side and avoiding the little ridge, Klaus let the cow pony head straight up the long slant. Jessie's mind was on the impromptu race more than the terrain; she was letting Sun pick his own way.

Belatedly, Jessie suddenly realized with a start that they'd come farther from the main house than she'd thought. More importantly, she remembered that on the downside of the slope they were now mounting one of the cowhands had discovered a long strip of jimsonweed. The Circle Star foreman had reported to her that he'd ordered the strip of poisonous growth to be fenced, in order to keep the range steers from grazing on it, until the roundup was over and the hands would have time to grub it out.

Raising her voice she called, "Klaus! Turn your mount! There's a fence at the bottom of this slope!"

Klaus was already near the crest of the rise. He turned to wave in reply to Jessie's voice, but it was obvious that he had not heard her warning, for he made no effort to wheel his horse or to rein in. He reached the top of the slope and almost at once disappeared as his cow pony plunged down the opposite side of the ridge. Jessie dug her heels into Sun's flanks, but the big palomino was already moving at the greatest speed he could muster as he neared the crest.

Only minutes passed before Sun reached the top of the hump that broke the flat expanse of level prairie, but by the time Jessie could look down the opposite slope she saw at once that the damage she'd feared had been done.

Klaus was sitting sidewise in his saddle, bending forward, his arms extended to allow his hands to close around the calf of his leg. As she drew closer she could see small trickles of blood oozing between his fingers, while on the flank of his horse narrow dark streaks of blood were also visible. Though the distance between them was not great, Jessie did not rein in, but again and again drummed her bootheels against Sun's heaving flanks in her haste to reach the injured man.

"Are you hurt badly, Klaus?" she called as she came within easy speaking distance.

"It is nothing," he called back. His collision with the fence had obviously agitated him, for as he went on, his usually excellent English was phrased in the Geremanic style. "A few scratches, no more. It is that I did not the fence see in time to wheel, and I could not quickly enough the horse rein in."

As brief as their exchange had been, Jessie was pulling Sun to a halt beside Klaus almost before he'd finished speaking. She glanced at his hands, clasped around his calf, and saw that blood was still welling between his fingers.

"It's not what I'd call nothing," she said. "From the way you're bleeding, I'd say your leg needs attention at once."

"It hurts very little," Klaus assured her. "A small pain now and then, but that will not bother me greatly."

"That leg should be tended to at once," Jessie insisted. "I know the kind of a cut barbwire can make, and it's a good two-hour ride back to the main house. There's not—" She stopped short and a thoughtful frown flitted across her face as she went on. "There is a place closer. One of our line shacks is only a mile or so from here. It'll have disinfectant and a roll of bandage in it."

"My own fault it is," Klaus said as Jessie began untying the big bandana that she wore as a neckerchief over the collar of her blouse. "I should not so careless have been."

"Nonsense!" she replied. She'd freed the bandana and was folding it in wide strips to form a bandage. "Pull up the leg of your trousers so I can wrap this around your calf and stop your bleeding."

Klaus began tugging at the fabric of his trousers and by the time Jessie had finished folding the big kerchief into a wide strip he had bared the wound in his calf. Jessie looked at the opened gash closely, examining it with the quick understanding look of one who'd seen many such lacerations before.

There were two or three small raw scratches on the middle area of Klaus's calf, between the ankle and knee, but in the muscle a clean-edged slit almost three inches long was bleeding freely. The wound sliced in a diagonal across Klaus's calf muscle and looked as though it had been inflicted by a butcher's well-honed knife.

37

"It's a clean cut," Jessie said as she pushed his blood-soaked sock down to his ankle. "But even if it's a makeshift, this bandage will keep you from bleeding while we're riding to the line shack, and I can do a better job there."

She placed the center of the folded bandana directly over the bleeding cut and wound the narrow strip of cotton fabric around Klaus's leg, then tied it off with a neat and virtually slip-proof square knot. By the time she'd completed the knot a wet red stain was showing on the makeshift bandage, but the blot it formed did not grow any larger than a silver dollar.

"You make a bandage as skillfully as might a surgeon," Klaus commented. "And now that my little cut no longer bleeds, I no longer feel any pain from it."

"I'm glad you're not hurting," Jessie said. "But we don't want to waste any time getting to the line shack. Let's move as fast as we can, while the blood on that bandana is still wet. If gets dry it'll stick and hurt you pretty badly when I take it off. Besides, I want to put some permanganate on the cut before it scabs over, to keep it from getting infected."

"I have yet no feeling of pain," Klaus told her. "I can ride without difficulty."

"Good," Jessie said as she swung into the saddle and reined Sun around. "But let's not waste any more time. Follow me, Klaus. I'm going to ride around this stand of loco weed and take the shortest way to the line shack."

★

Chapter 4

"This line shack of which you speak, Jessie, what is it, please?" Klaus frowned as he and Jessie started moving. "Before now, of such a thing I have not heard."

"It's just a small one-room shanty where the hands who're riding herd can cook a meal and spend a night or two without having to go all the way back to the bunkhouse," Jessie explained. "There are a half-dozen of them scattered across the Circle Star range."

"Ah." Klaus nodded. "A cottage, you mean."

"Hardly that," she smiled. "Line houses are just big enough to hold a bed and a little stove and some airtights to tide over a hand for a meal or two. But they're awfully welcome to a wrangler who's caught in a rainstorm and needs a place to shelter, or to stir up a meal when he can't leave a raw herd long enough to ride as far as the cookhouse."

Klaus shook his head as he said, "Again I am astonished by all the appurtances you have on your amazing ranch."

"Most of the really big ranches have these appurtances, as you call them," Jessie went on. "But they're all designed to save time. Just as you have, Klaus, ranch hands get hurt now and then, and have stomachaches, so we keep a little medical kit in each line shack. It doesn't have anything in it but a bottle of castor oil for a bad bellyache and a bottle of hydrogen peroxide and a roll of bandage for protecting cuts or bad scrapes."

"I can understand now." He nodded. "And again I am impressed by the way in which you keep functioning in so businesslike fashion an operation of such size."

As Jessie had promised, the little one-room line shack, its weather-grayed boards outlined sharply against the green of the range in the bright Texas sunshine, was less than a quarter-hour ride from the patch of fenced jimsonweed. She reined in when they reached it and dropped out of Sun's saddle, then extended a hand to help Klaus dismount.

"Help I do not yet need," he told her. His tone was defensively stiff.

Though Klaus lurched a bit when he put his full weight on his injured leg, he recovered quickly and followed Jessie to the door of the small shanty. His jaw dropped when she opened the door, and disbelief was in his voice when he spoke.

"You do not lock the little house?" he frowned.

"Of course not, none of the ranches do." Surprise tinged Jessie's voice as she answered, then she added, "There's never anything in a line house that a thief would take time to steal. Besides that, it's not very handy for cowhands to carry big key rings around with them when they're out on the range, Klaus."

They were entering the line shack as Jessie spoke. Klaus flicked his eyes around the cramped little room. It contained a narrow bed, only a little wider than a cot, a pair of chairs, and a small potbellied stove. A board shelf fastened to the wall beneath the shack's single window obviously served as a table, for a pair of plates and a little clutter of table utensils rested on it. A second shelf with a few cloth-wrapped bundles on it occupied the corner behind the door. On the floor beneath the shelf a water bucket was upended.

"Sit down and roll up your trouser leg on the one that's hurt," Jessie told Klaus as she pushed the door closed in order to get better access to the shelf holding the bundles. She began feeling the packages and lifted down the third one she tried. "This one has to have the peroxide in it," she went on, speaking now to herself as much as to her companion. She unrolled the cloth to disclose a large brown bottle. Holding it up to the light that flooded in through the shack's window, she nodded with satisfaction and stepped up to the bed.

Klaus had settled down on the bed and was following Jessie's instructions, rolling up the shreds of torn fabric that sheathed his injured leg. He loosened the knot of the bandana and started to unwind it, but the clotted blood that had soaked through the bandana's folds was now dry and the fabric was sticking to his leg. Klaus winced as he tugged gently at the loose ends of the kerchief.

"Wait a minute, Klaus," Jessie said as she kneeled on the narrow strip of floorboards between the bed and the wall. "Let me pour some of this peroxide on the bandana. It'll soak the dried blood out of the cloth and then we can just lift it away without hurting you."

"I can stand the pain, Jessie; it is not too great," Klaus told her. "But do what you think is best."

Jessie was already pressing the peroxide bottle's top on the injured leg above the bandana. She tilted it carefully to let a small trickle of the liquid run down to the dangling kerchief. Hunkering back on her heels, she set the bottle on the floor beside her and took one end of the folded bandana in each hand.

"Give the peroxide a minute to soak in, then the bandage will come free without any trouble," she said.

"I can feel the cut tingling a bit." Klaus nodded. "But it is not at all painful. Do you add a doctor's work to your other responsibilities here on your ranch, Jessie?"

"Somebody has to take care of the small cuts and scrapes the hands are always getting," she replied. "But generally they'll do their doctoring or ask Steve or the cook to help them."

By this time the kerchief's fabric was darkening rapidly to a rusty black as the liquid soaked into it. Jessie began tugging gently at one end, then at the other. Wetted by the peroxide, the impromptu bandage soon gave way in response to her carefully applied pulls, and she leaned forward to examine the injured leg. Klaus was bending down to look at the same time that Jessie moved, and their heads collided with a none-too-gentle bump. Klaus raised his head as Jessie dropped back to sit on her heels. They stared at one another for a moment; then both began to laugh.

"I'm sorry," Jessie said as their chuckles subsided. "I was too interested in seeing how your injury was to pay much attention to anything else."

"So was I," Klaus told her. "I hope I didn't hurt you."

"No damage was done," Jessie assured him. She went on, "I need to look at your leg closely, so—"

"Don't worry," he broke in. "This time I will keep my head from in your way getting."

Picking up the bandana that had already done service as a bandage, Jessie soaked a clean corner of its fabric with peroxide and swabbed at the skin around the slash, then carefully wiped away the trickle of fresh blood that was seeping from the cut. The barbwire had made a clean gash in the long, bulging muscle of Klaus's calf, but the sharp barb had not been long enough to slash deeply. She could see that the wound was not deep enough to have a permanent effect on the muscle's flexing, though using the leg would probably cause Klaus some discomfort for several days.

"It's not as bad as I was afraid it would be," she told him. "It could be called either a very deep scratch or a shallow cut. I've seen enough wounds like this to know a little bit about them. You'll have to favor this leg a little while, long enough for the cut to start healing. It'll itch for a few days, and the muscle will probably be stiff for a week or more, but your leg's not permanently damaged."

"That's certainly good news," he said. "I was afraid I'd be an invalid for a while and would have to stay in bed and a great deal of inconvenience cause you. You make me so happy, Jessie, that out of joy and thanks I must kiss you."

To Jessie's surprise, Klaus cradled her chin in one hand, pulled her to him with his free arm and bent forward to find her lips with his. He did not release her after their lips had met, and after a moment or two had passed Jessie felt the tip of his questing tongue touch her lips.

Somewhat to her own surprise Jessie found herself responding. Klaus's sudden and unexpected soft caress was

43

bringing about a rekindling of the desires that she was accustomed to pushing aside and ignoring during her stays on the Circle Star. She thrust her tongue tip forward to meet Klaus's softly silent advance. They held their kiss for several moments, exchanging tongue caresses, until finally their lack of breath forced them to part.

Both Klaus and Jessie had closed their eyes during the long kiss. Now they opened them, and exchanged glances, their eyes only inches apart.

"There is little chance that here we would be interrupted, no?" Klaus's question was whispered softly, but the tone of his voice was urgent.

Jessie shook her head and said, "No. The range riders won't be coming back to this part of the ranch for several days."

"Tell me, why then we should hesitate?" he asked. The urgency in his words was stronger now. "If you have binding ties to another . . . " His voice trailed off on the question, and when Jessie shook her head, he went on, "From the moment I saw you, I have wanted to hold you and caress you."

"Do, then," she invited.

Klaus pulled her to him and their lips met again. When at last their kiss ended he began brushing his moist lips along Jessie's soft cheeks. His caresses trailed down to the smooth white pillar of her throat, and when he reached the loose, wide collar of her blouse he pushed it aside, to let his tongue and lips find the sensitive hollows between the base of her neck and her shoulder.

Jessie was aroused now, all her senses urging her to accept Klaus's caresses to the fullest. She leaned back when his fingers sought the buttons of her blouse and undid them, and shrugged her shoulders to help him free her from the blouse. His head moved down until he could find the budded tips of her firm, generous breasts. Then he began rubbing the ruby-hued buds with his lips and lightly rasping tongue.

For several moments Jessie luxuriated in the sensation his caresses summoned, then she stirred with restless impatience. Klaus recognized her signal. He rose and began to unbutton the fly of his trousers. He'd succeded in loosening only one button before Jessie rolled off the narrow bed and stood beside him. Without speaking they began playing the sort of game that fascinates new lovers, helping one another to undress.

They said little but let their hands talk for them while their lips were busy with kisses. After Jessie's blouse had been tossed aside, Klaus devoted his attention to her full, upstanding breasts, kissing their warmly resilient buds and at the same time tugging at her skirt. At last the skirt slipped free, and he let it fall in a heap on the floor. He wasted no time in finding and pulling the drawstring of her short pantaloons and sending them to join her skirt.

Jessie's hands had been busy as well, her fingers working at Klaus's fly, releasing the buttons of his trousers. She undid the final button and tugged at the trousers until she succeeded in pulling them down, then she let them slide and crumple around his feet. When they dropped away, the erection that had been bulging his clothing was freed to spring up, and Jessie fondled and stroked him gently until she realized that he was growing restless with mounting tension.

"Now, Klaus," she whispered between kisses. "Now!"

Wrapping his arms around her, Klaus lifted her from the floor and edged closer to the narrow cot that served as a bed. Jessie brought up her legs and embraced his hips with her thighs. She clung with one arm across his shoulders while she placed him, then fell back on the cot as he completed his penetration with a single fierce lunge.

As Klaus began stroking, Jessie sighed and lay supine for a moment or two, content to accept and enjoy her lover's quick lusty thrusts as he drove into her. She realized very quickly that in his eagerness Klaus was giving little thought to her needs. Locking her ankles at his back she drew him into her as he thrust, then clasped her legs to clamp Klaus with her strong thighs. Then, rotating her hips gently, she held him buried for several moments at the end of each lunging penetration while they lay without moving.

Time no longer mattered to them now. They prolonged their embrace without regard for the passing moments until at last their mutual pleasure mounted to its peak. Jessie signaled her readiness by sprawling her thighs as widely as possible and releasing the pressure she'd been exerting with the silken columns of her legs. Klaus quickly read her signal and began driving to their climax.

He began thrusting fiercely again, and Jessie matched his swiftening strokes, bucking upward each time he drove in. At last the rapture they'd been seeking swept over them in a final burst of furious thrashing on the narrow cot, and they shuddered with ecstatic sighs into the final climax.

For several moments they did not stir but lay sprawled in luxuriously limp exhaustion. Jessie was the first to move. She stirred and rolled her shoulders from side to side. Klaus bent to kiss her lips, and they held their embrace for a few moments longer with their lips pressed together. At last Klaus sighed and rose from the narrow cot to stand beside her.

"Did I succeed in pleasing you, Jessie?" he asked.

"Very much so," she nodded. She was rising from the cot as she replied. "But we'll please one another again, and more comfortably, in my bedroom tonight."

"This is what I had hoped you might say," he told her. "Then do we now end our time of looking at your great ranch and to your main house return?"

"Of course. We'll get there in time for supper, and Ki will have finished going through Alex's files by now, so we'll at least have a place we can start from. We shouldn't have too much trouble in coming to an agreement."

"We'll have plenty of time to talk privately before Klaus comes down for supper, Ki," Jessie said. She and Ki were sitting in the study of the Circle Star's big main house. "The first thing I'd like to do is find out all there is to know about that promissory note that Alex gave Gustaf Reiden."

"That's something we might never know," Ki told her. "And I don't suppose Klaus was inclined to pass on any more information during your ride?"

Jessie shook her head as she said, "No. But the little cut he got on his leg and having to ride to the nearest line shack to put a bandage on it got in the way of all the questions I had in mind to ask him. I've been hoping you ran across something in those old files that might explain why and how Alex gave Gustaf Reiden a note like that."

"Unfortunately, I didn't find a thing about the note," Ki replied. "Alex didn't keep very detailed records when he was first getting started."

"Yes, I've found that out." She nodded. "But even the few notes he made of what he'd done, where he'd been, things of that sort, might turn out to be helpful."

"I'm sure you've thought of asking young Reiden some more questions."

"It's possible that he doesn't have any more to pass on." She frowned. "But in the little time I've had to think about it, I don't believe it would have any legal standing. Not that I want to make a big issue of it, of course. I'd much rather just deal with Klaus as though the note doesn't exist."

"That may be the easiest way to handle things," Ki said slowly. "But wouldn't it be better for us to come up with some way of getting rid of it?"

"I've thought about that a bit," Jessie replied. "But I don't think there's a way to do it quickly. Right at the moment, I'm more inclined to stretch every point possible. That doesn't mean I intend to ignore the fact that the note exists."

"That may not be easy to do," Ki cautioned her. "But something might turn up that would give us an idea about a fresh approach."

"Let's just try to avoid discussing it," Jessie said. "We'll see what develops when we've talked with Klaus a bit more this evening after dinner."

"Your chef must very talented be, Jessie," Klaus said as he walked with Jessie and Ki across the small stretch of land that separated the Circle Star's cookshack from the main house, "to provide such excellent meals with resources which must here in such an isolated place be small indeed."

"Just because we live a good distance from a large town doesn't mean that our resources are small." Jessie smiled.

"Cookie orders pretty much anything he pleases from the big wholesale grocery houses in San Antonio and Fort Worth, and if he's feeling notional, from New York and San Francisco."

"Then that explains it!" Klaus exclaimed. Shaking his head, he went on, "I have seen too little of your vast country, Jessie. Living in my crowded homeland, I still do not realize that the style in which you live must be so very different from ours in the fatherland."

"I'll admit, it takes a bit of adjustment." Jessie nodded. "But after you've gotten used to living in America you come to take distances for granted."

They'd reached the sprawling main house now, and as they went inside Ki asked, "Are you and Klaus still planning to discuss the business that's brought him here, Jessie? Or did your day tire you too much?"

"I think Klaus is the one to decide that," Jessie replied. "He's the one who came back with an injured leg after a fairly busy day."

"My leg does not at all bother me," Klaus said quickly. "I am quite prepared to go on with our unfinished business."

"We'll go on into the study, then." Jessie nodded. "Knowing you, Ki, I'm sure you've got everything ready."

"Certainly," Ki told her. "Everything's in order. We can sit right down and begin."

After they'd settled into chairs in the big, friendly room, Jessie looked at Klaus and said, "You know what my main concern is, I'm sure."

"Of course," he nodded. "The strange promissory note from your father which my father holds. The coal for which

49

being in America is my main purpose is to you not as important as the note must be."

"You're quite right, of course," Jessie agreed. "It isn't that I'm at all worried about your family even thinking about using it to acquire all the Starbuck properties. It's just a loose end to your present purpose, Klaus. But to me—well, if you've put yourself in my shoes, as I'm sure you have, you know that promissory note could be devastating."

"That, too, I understand," Klaus said. "Even though you know it now presents no danger."

"Things change very rapidly sometimes," Jessie pointed out.

"They do," he nodded. "And of the problem you must be facing, my father is well aware. He has proposed that I offer you what he would consider a permanent solution."

Jessie was silent for a moment, and a small frown formed on her face as she said, "Apparently your father is as concerned as I am about the strange situation that Alex's promissory note could create."

"He is, and I assure you, Jessie, that his feelings I share."

"Let's hear the solution he's come up with, then," Jessie suggested.

"It is not easy and simple," Klaus told her.

"Very few things are in real life," Jessie smiled.

"Of course," Klaus agreed. "Very well. His suggestion is that we go to Alaska together and inspect the area where the coal deposits are located. You and I will then agree on a fair price for them, which I am authorized to pay. Upon payment, I will also surrender to you the promissory note. Then we will have the coal, and of all worry you will be free."

Jessie did not hesitate. Even the prospect of having to travel to Alaska did not deter her. The offer was even more than she'd hoped for. In spite of the long friendship between her father and Gustaf Reiden, she'd been prepared to accept an offer to swap the promissory note for the coal deposits.

"We have a deal, Klaus," she nodded. "Ki and I will be glad to go with you to Alaska. Just tell me when you want to start."

★

Chapter 5

"It's been the better part of a week now, and we're still the only passengers who get out of bed at daylight," Jessie said to Ki as he came up to join her. She was standing at the apex of the rail in the prow of the side-wheel steamship *Nancy Belle,* the early morning sea breeze tossing her long blond hair. "But where is Klaus this morning?

"He'll be along presently," Ki replied. A smile spread over his face as he went on, "Klaus wasn't at the Circle Star long enough to get accustomed to starting the day at sunup."

"Or going to bed early, either," Jessie said. "He tried to persuade me to stay and dance in the main salon after supper. That's what most of the passengers did; the rest were at the gambling tables. I begged off, though. The sea air always makes me sleepy the first few nights out."

"I suppose most of our fellow passengers will be dancing

all night for the rest of our voyage." Ki nodded. "As closely as I can tell, all of them seem to feel that this is going to be their last bit of freedom before we get to Alaska. I'm sure that's why they stay up dancing or gambling until long after midnight."

"Probably," Jessie agreed. "And I'm sure that very few of the *Nancy Belle*'s passengers are used to getting up as early as we do on the Circle Star."

"We've remarked before that all of them look citified," Ki went on. "Don't you imagine it's the thought of going to what they've heard of as being a wild, untamed wilderness that's making them feel they're entitled to a final fling?"

"You're pretty certain to be right," Jessie said. Then she went on, "But do you know, Ki, it's been such a long time since we've been on any ship bigger than a river steamer that I'd almost forgotten how restful ocean travel in a big vessel can be."

"I've never found it as restful as you seem to, Jessie. Perhaps the big new ships they call ocean liners are restful, but I've never made a voyage in one of them. Remember, most of the sailing I've done has been between Japan and Korea or China, short trips in sampans or junks."

"And as you know, all my sailing's been along the coast or up the big rivers," Jessie said. "The Circle Star, together with all the other businesses that Alex left me, has kept both of us too busy to travel for pleasure."

As they talked idly, neither Jessie nor Ki took their eyes off the endless vista of gently dimpling green ocean waves as the *Nancy Belle* wallowed steadily ahead, leaving in its wake a wide roiled stream of bubbles from its twin side wheels.

"Perhaps the ocean fascinates me because we're so land-bound on the Circle Star," Jessie went on with a thoughtful frown. "But just traveling on coastal ships like this one, I've learned that the Pacific Ocean can look harmless and peaceful the way it does now, and then within a very few minutes we might find ourselves in the middle of a raging storm."

"I'd certainly hate to see that, as crowded as this boat is," Ki went on. "Because that new bunch of gold strikes we read about in the newspapers during the few days we spent in San Francisco has pretty obviously started another Alaskan gold rush."

"I think Alaskan gold rushes are something like the seven-year itch," Jessie smiled. "They break out on a pretty regular schedule."

"You may be right," Ki agreed. "From what I remember Alex telling me, he was in at least three, and none of them were more than a few years apart."

"He always said that he got his real start in Alaska." Jessie nodded. "And that an old prospector, whose name he never did know, gave him the advice that led to him going up to the northern part, the Yukon I suppose it's called, where there weren't so many gold seekers, instead of prospecting in the easier territory at the southern end of the peninsula."

"It's going to be interesting to see whether Klaus adapts to Alaska," Ki went on. "He certainly didn't have any trouble adjusting to the Circle Star."

"I'm sure he'll manage," Jessie said. "He seems to be one of those people who have the ability to—"

She broke off as a loud metallic cracking sounded above the gentle susurrus of the steamship's bow wave. It was followed by several higher-pitched pops of metal giving way to stress. The big paddle wheel on the side of the vessel where Jessie and Ki were standing began moving more and more slowly, and the ship started veering to one side, leaving the straight course it had been following.

"There's something wrong with that paddle wheel, Ki," Jessie said as she turned to look at the small section of the huge wheel that was visible between the sea's surface and the bottom of the wide semicircular metal hood that encased it. "It's the only place that noise we just heard could've come from, and it looks to me as though this boat's about to stop."

"Yes, it is," he agreed. Then he pointed to the ship's wake and went on, "It also explains why we're beginning to travel in a curve instead of a straight line, as we were a minute or so ago. Look how that froth in the boat's wake is curving around."

"Our ship seems to be having troubles, no?" Klaus Reiden asked as he came up to join them. "I was to the dining salon going, thinking to find you there at breakfast. Then I hear the strange noise from this direction coming and look to see you."

While they were talking the noise of the ship's engine changed its rhythmic tempo. The steady susurrus of its sound began to fade. Then it dropped to a whisper and stopped completely, and the only sound that could now be heard was the splashing of waves against the vessel's hull.

"There's certainly something wrong," Jessie said. "But I'm sure that the crew can fix whatever it is."

As though her words had been a summons, two men emerged from the pilot house that rose above the passenger

56

accommodations deck and came hurrying toward the rail where Jessie, Ki and Klaus were standing. They recognized only one of the trio, the vessel's commander.

"Miss Starbuck." He nodded. "I hope this little problem we seem to be having isn't worrying you too much."

"Of course not, Captain Farrell," Jessie replied. "I'm sure that you and your sailors are quite capable of handling any trouble the ship might have."

"That's why we've stopped," Farrell said. "Angus, here —our chief engineer—is sure that he's already figured out what the trouble is."

"That I have," the engineer said. "There's only the one thing that could be wrong."

"And this thing, it can be made right?" Klaus asked.

"Oh, aye," Angus nodded. " 'Tis just one single bolt that's gang aglee. 'Tis a muckle big bolt called the stay bolt that runs through the paddle wheel hubs and holds them on their shafts."

"To me, what you say is words that mean nothing." Klaus frowned. "Please, be good enough to explain."

"Weel, now," Angus went on, "the shafts are what turn the paddle wheels. They're the connection tae the steam engine, that's where they get the power tae make the paddles turn, d'ye see."

"Now that you make it clear, I understand it," Klaus nodded. "But go more ahead and tell me where it is that the engine has downbroken."

"Not the engine," Angus said quickly. "What I'm sure's happened is the stay bolt on this wheel wasna tightened firm, or mayhap it broke and just slipped free. All we need tae do now is tae push in a new bolt and tighten it firm and solid, then we'll be on our way again."

"And you have the new bolt to push in and tighten, as you've just said?" Jessie asked.

"Aye, that I do." Angus nodded. "Richt at the noo my helper's going around looking in the crew for a pair of good swimmers tae do the job."

"Isn't it sort of a dangerous one?" Jessie asked.

" 'Tisn't dangerous, but 'tis cramped-tight space under the wheel cover," Angus replied. "A mon could fall in all tae easy, and the seawater's muckle cold. But soon as I find the hands I need and see to them putting in the new bolt and drawing it firm, we'll be on our way again."

"I wish it was as easy as you make it sound, Chief," said the sailor who'd arrived just in time to hear the chief engineer's statement. "I've just finished the job you sent me to do. I've talked to every hand above and below decks, and there's not a one in the whole bunch that'll admit they can swim a stroke."

"Noo, how can that be?" Angus asked, turning to the captain. "What sort of sailor is it that's not able to swim?"

"You ought to know the answer to that, Angus," Farrell replied. "We've both heard the waterfront stories going around about the number of ships beached up in Alaska, a ship every few miles between Cordova and Seward and along the shore of Norton Sound, because their hands have deserted to go inland and look for gold. The sailors have jumped ship and become prospectors."

"Then it looks like a job for you and me, Captain," Angus told the ship's commander. "If you'll come along, I'll show you what needs to be done and we'll just do it."

"I can't take on that sort of job," the captain protested. "I've got a shoulder full of lead left over from the war. That's why I'm not still wearing U.S. Navy sideboards.

With only one useful arm, I'd be a drag on you, maybe a dangerous one."

Jessie, Ki and Klaus had been following the discussion between the ship's officers. Before either of them could speak again, Ki broke in.

"I'll give you what help you might need, Angus," he volunteered. "I suppose you'd call me a landlubber, but I can swim about as well as the next man, and I know how to thread a bolt on a nut, if that's all you need done."

"And if more help you need, I will with you be glad to go," Klaus said quickly. "It is better that too much help you will have instead of not enough, yes?"

"Aye, an extra pair of hands will be good tae have along," Angus agreed. "All richt. It's settled, then." Turning to the sailor, he went on, "You go down tae the engine room. Tell one of the stokers you want the big bolt that's in a box in the parts locker, and a pair of wrenches that'll mate to the head and the nut. Bring them back here to me and don't waste any time going or coming."

"I don't suppose there's any way to fix that paddle wheel without you men going in the water?" Farrell asked.

"Nae way at all," the engineer replied, shaking his head. "A mon ten feet tall micht have the reach he'll need tae fit the bolt wi'out being in the sea, but we've nae got a man ten feet tall aboard this auld tub."

Ki broke the momentary silence that settled over the little group following Angus's answer. He turned to the chief engineer and asked, "Just what is it that needs to be done to make this repair?"

"What we have here is a wheel and a hub," Angus explained. " 'Tis a mickle like a wheel on a wagon that's fitted to an axle, but 'tis bigger by ten times or more. Now, there's holes been drilled through the axle's end and the hub of the wheel. We slide in the new bolt and put on the nut, then tighten it wi' a monkey wrench. That's the full and all of it."

"And you'll be able to show Klaus and me exactly what to do?" Ki pressed.

"It'll be easier showing you after we get down in the wheelhouse than tae try and tell you standing up here on deck," Angus replied. "Just remember ye'll have to work fast, because that water's going to be ice cold."

"This we can I think endure," Klaus volunteered. He turned to Ki, his brows raised questioningly. "Is it not so, Ki?"

"If we have to work fast, we ought to be able to." Ki nodded. He glanced at Angus and went on, "We're ready when you are."

"Follow behind me, then," the engineer said. "I'll show ye both the places where ye'll be working, and answer any questions ye may hae to ask. After that, 'twill be up tae the two of ye."

"I hope you won't mind if I go along?" Jessie asked. "I'll be careful to stay out of your way and just look and listen."

"Aye, if you've a mind to." Angus nodded. "Though there's going tae be little enough tae see."

With Jessie, Ki and Klaus following, the engineer led them along the row of cabins that rose from the narrow strip of decking that ran around the vessel's perimeter. They reached a spot amidships where the walkway ended at the paddle-wheel housing, a big enclosed half-circle of painted and gilt-decorated sheet metal. The housing curved upward from the waterline to the top of the cabin tier, and when they reached it Angus waved them to a halt.

"Ye'll be working from inside the wheel housing," he explained. "The light'll nae be gude, but 'twill be bright enough for ye tae see what ye're doing."

As Angus spoke he produced a ring of jangling keys from his pocket and selected one which he fitted into a keyhole that was almost invisible among the decorative swirls and curlicues that were painted on the wheel housing. As he turned the key and swung the narrow door open, Ki and Klaus and Jessie huddled up behind him, looking into the cavernous arched cavity.

After their eyes had adjusted to the dimness of the semicircular enclosure, they could see the ironwork skeleton that supported the big, closely spaced wooden paddles. Had the iron members forming the framework been small and made of sheer gossamer threads, the paddle wheel's supporting structure might have been taken for the web of some monstrous and industrious spider.

In the middle of the arc's flat base the paddle wheel's center hub protruded from the ship's side almost at the level of the deck. The hub was as big around as a large man's waist, and sturdy lengths of squared timbers radiated from it to support the steel rings of the massive paddle wheel. Around the wheel's twin rims the flat, thick paddles were set. They, too, were braced with lengths of timber to hold them in place while they splashed down on the water's surface.

Between the two massive circles of steel the paddles stretched. These were made of wood, pairs of boards five or six inches thick, with iron-framed ends, braced by iron straps in the center. The two or three bottom paddles were almost hidden under the riffled surface of the water, their tops barely visible in the dim light of the wheel housing.

At the center of the paddle wheel the hub was veiled in

gloom, but after their eyes had adjusted to the dim half-twilight, half-darkness of the enclosure, Jessie and her companions could make out its form and could see that it was a casting of iron or steel that circled the end of the huge drive shaft that protruded from the vessel's side.

"Just what is it we're supposed to do now?" Ki asked, turning to Angus after he'd completed his inspection.

"If ye'll look close enough nearby the end of the drive-shaft, ye'll see the holes that's been drilled in it. Now, they're set to match another hole drilled all the way through the hub. That deckhand's bringing a big round length of steel; we call it the pin. It'll span all the holes, and stick out far enough tae put a nut on it. It's the pin that's been lost, d'ye see? And it's what counts, because it makes the paddle wheel turn when the shaft goes round. The pin holds them taegether and makes the wheel turn wi' the shaft."

"What keeps the pin from falling out?" Klaus asked.

"Why, it's shouldered at the top and threaded at the bottom," Angus answered. "What's happened is that the old pin either got sheared off or lost the nut. Then it dropped free. It's your job the noo tae put in the new pin, then put the nut on it and draw it tight."

"That means the holes in the wheel and the axle have to be lined up," Ki said.

"Aye," Angus agreed. "That's why ye're both here, and why I'm here meself. I'll turn the wheel; the two of ye'll put in the bolt. Decide between yourselves which of ye'll fit it and push it through that hole in the shaft and which one will put on the nut and draw it tight once it's set in place."

Klaus looked questioningly at Ki, who shrugged and said, "You stay down here to balance and tighten. I'll scramble up to where I can get to the top of the hole. Angus has already decided he'll be the one to turn the paddle wheel."

"Agreed." Klaus nodded. He extended his hand to Angus, who passed him the long blued-steel bolt. Working carefully, Klaus unscrewed the nut and handed it up to Ki. He went on, "And as soon as the pin you have fitted, the nut I will attach."

"Aye, that's what's needed," Angus agreed. "I'll turn the wheel slow, so you'll have nae trouble sliding the pin through."

"You can't turn that big paddle wheel by yourself," Jessie said. "I'll help you."

" 'Tis not a job you should take on," Angus snapped. "We're doing men's work, lass!"

"Just the same, I'm going to stay," Jessie replied, her voice firm. "And if you need help, I'll be here ready to lend you another pair of hands."

"Aye, suit yourself, then." Angus's voice showed his reluctance. "But stand out of our way now, and let's get on with the job."

Only moments had passed while Angus was explaining the task facing them, and the compartment that formed the paddle wheel's cover was shielded from the wind. However, while they'd talked the chill rising from the water's surface had been at work. Within the arched enclosure the cold air grew steadily cooler as Angus and Ki and Klaus took their positions and Jessie moved closer to the spot where Angus was bracing himself to heave against one of the massive wheel's spokes.

By the time they were placed satisfactorily, the chill was sinking into their muscles and stiffening their hands. From her position on the narrow ledge beside Angus, Jessie looked up at Ki and Klaus as they clambered up to the great squared timbers, held together by thick iron straps, through which the hubshafts connecting the huge paddle wheels passed.

"Slide your bolt into the hub easy, now," Angus called to Ki. "It'll likely push up against the axle, and when it does, I'll need tae turn the wheel slow to line up the bolt wi' the hole in the shaft."

Ki answered with a gesture to signify he understood. He was bracing himself in place on the cross-timber in order to have both hands free to manipulate the bolt when he began threading it through the massive timber forming the shaft. In a satisfactory position at last, he began pushing the threaded end of the metal rod into the paddle wheel's huge hub. The watchers saw the rod sink in a few inches, and stop.

"Turn the wheel just a bit more!" Ki called. "The bolt's started, but I can't push it all the way through yet."

"Aye," Angus called back. "Steady, now, while I put me shoulder to the job!"

Swiveling as best he could on his narrow perch, Angus got a shoulder on one of the big wheel's cross-members and began to press. The wheel did not budge.

Jessie said quickly, "Wait, Angus! I'll add my weight to yours and maybe we can get the wheel to move!"

Backing up to the paddle wheel's nearest spoke, Jessie braced herself and pushed. Slowly and with great reluctance, the wheel budged. It had moved only an inch or two when Ki called urgently, "Stop now! I feel the bolt sinking in!"

"Hold it steady, lads!" Angus called out.

Turning as best she could, Jessie gripped the wheel's nearest spoke and heaved backward. The rough timber was biting painfully into her fingers when Klaus and Ki spoke at almost the same moment.

"Stop!" Ki called.

"*Sehr gut!*" Klaus shouted only a second or two later. "The bolt end I have in my hand! Hold steady the wheel! I am now the nut attaching!"

With the combined efforts of Jessie and Angus, the almost imperceptible movement of the massive wheel was halted. Only a moment passed before Klaus raised his voice again.

"It is finished!" he shouted joyfully. "Is tight the bolt! Now the ship can once more move!"

"That's the best news yet," Jessie exclaimed. "Now let's all get back up on deck where we can relax and get warm. And I can't think of anything I'd rather look at than the wake of this ship when it starts on its course again!"

★

Chapter 6

"Why didn't the clerk in your booking office in San Francisco tell us about this when we were buying our tickets?" Jessie asked the ship's purser.

She made no effort to keep the annoyance she felt from showing in her voice. Ki and Klaus were standing a bit away from Jessie and the purser, and in accordance with their prearranged plan, they remained silent.

"More than likely whoever arranged for your passage didn't even know that a change would be necessary, Miss Starbuck," the ship's officer replied. "Down in the States people don't always understand Alaskan waterways. They don't realize that the inland passage ends here at Cook's Anchorage, and if you're heading for Nome or Barrow, you must be on a vessel that's bound through the Bering Straits."

"Someone in your office in San Francisco must certainly

have known the difference," Jessie insisted. "But nothing at all was said about it. Now, without advance warning of any sort, we suddenly find that we're expected—though forced would be a better word—that we'll have to wait here several days where there's just a skeleton of a town and change to another ship that'll take us on to where we've been expecting to be taken by this one."

"It's just a case of human error," the purser said apologetically. "But you'll only have three or four days—a week at most—to wait for the vessel that'll be taking you and your party to the up-country."

"And where are we supposed to stay while we're waiting those three or four days or a week?" Jessie frowned. "From what I've heard about Alaska since we sailed from San Francisco, in just about any town you might name there are more people than there are places where they can find shelter."

"At least I can relieve you of worrying about a place to stay," he said. "Our agents know how hard it is to find accommodations up here, so our line provides a few rooms at most of the ports where our ships put in regularly."

"I'm not as interested in having accommodations here as I am in continuing our trip." Jessie frowned. "Perhaps you know of a boat or small ship that I can charter to take us the rest of the way?"

"I'm not all that well-acquainted with this port, Miss Starbuck," the purser answered. "My job's with the passengers. Now, if you'd like me to, I'll ask the captain or first mate about a boat you could charter, but I've heard enough dinner table talk to know that there's rarely a vessel up here at this time of year that's not been chartered for as much as a year in advance. Along the shoreline where the water's shallow ships can only get to land for about two months between freezes, and what with the hide hunters and the gold seekers there's just never enough vessels to go around."

"Not even in a busy port, such as I've heard this one to be?" Jessie frowned.

"Well, now, you were quite right a moment ago when you said that this isn't a town or a real port," the purser replied. "It's just a place where coastal ships can put in for a day or two. The harbor's well sheltered, but about all you'll find on shore is a hide warehouse and two or three stores and about that many rooming houses."

"I suppose it has a name?" Jessie asked. "I like to know where I'm stopping."

"Sailors started calling it Cook's Anchorage," the purser replied. "And I guess the name will stick. It might even grow into a town sometime, if gold prospectors and fugitives from the States keep coming to Alaska to hide from the law."

"Since we don't seem to any choice other than waiting here to change to another ship," Jessie said, "perhaps you'd better show us where we'll find these accommodations your firm has for passengers like us, who get stranded here."

"They're not right in the area here where most of the vessels put in," he told her. "It's a busy port at present; men are sleeping in day and night shifts in what few rooms there are to rent on shore. But our company's leased a river steamer that's broken down and waiting for some engine parts. The ship's the *Persephone,* and if you'd care to step out on deck with me, I'll point her out to you. She's at anchor about a hundred yards from the end of this dock, and she's almost a sister ship to the *Nancy Belle,* so you won't have any trouble recognizing her."

With the purser in the lead, Jessie, Ki and Klaus moved out to the deck. It was their first really clear view of the shore. Dusk had fallen while the *Nancy Belle* was still making its way up Cook Inlet, the wide inland passage they'd entered in the early dusk of the previous day. By the time the vessel had reached its destination all that had been visible beyond the wharf was a scanty speckling of lights on the shore.

Seeing it now in daylight, the land that rose away from the waterfront reminded Jessie of the raw, unsettled Texas country that lay between the southern fence line of the Circle Star and the Rio Grande. Though the earth here was bare of the prairie grass that covered even the scruffiest southwestern range, it stretched beyond the scattering of small shabby buildings in an unbroken sweep across a long upslope to the horizon. In the distance she could see the crest line of high hills rising in jagged edges against the incredibly bright sky.

In the foreground, only a short distance from the waterfront, there was a little settlement, its houses and buildings ending in a scattering of shanties on the gentle slope of the hill away from the shore. Unlike the nearest buildings, which faced one another across a wide, well-beaten stretch of the path, the smaller structures on the rising ground beyond the tidal flat were scattered willy-nilly and set in no pattern that indicated connecting streets.

Jessie and her companions had very little time to examine the terrain beyond the anchorage, for the purser led them to the ship's prow and pointed along the shore, to a side-wheel steamer that was nosed into a low bank at the water's edge. The vessel was a bit smaller than the one that had brought them from San Francisco.

"That's the *Persephone*," he said. "You'll have free berths on her until one of the coastal vessels that plies between here and the upland ports puts out on its next trip north to Nome and Barrow."

"Surely you must have some sort of idea when one of those ships is due," Jessie frowned.

"I'm afraid not," the purser replied. "I'm just guessing when I say three or four days. One of them might even be here tomorrow, but it certainly oughtn't be longer than a week."

"Well, that's something of a relief," Jessie said, her voice indicating that her irritation had been mollified somewhat by his reply. "And I suppose your accommodations will include providing our meals while we're waiting?"

"I'm afraid not. You'll surely understand that food's not as easy to come by up here in the north country as it is down in the States." He turned to point to one of the little clusters of buildings on the uphill trail leading from the waterfront as he went on, "There's a store up there. It'll likely have most everything you'll need to get along for a few days. Food and a cooking pot and things of that sort."

Ki was standing at Jessie's side. He'd been silent while she and the purser talked. Now he broke in to say, "Isn't a half loaf better than none, Jessie? At least we won't be forced to sleep on blankets spread on the beach while we're waiting for the other ship to get here."

"Yes, I suppose so." She nodded. Turning back to the purser, she went on, "I'm sure that you'll have our luggage moved to this boat we'll be staying on?"

"Of course," he replied. "In fact, I believe it's already been transferred." He groped in his jacket pocket for a moment and produced three keys. As he handed them to

Jessie, he went on, "These are pass keys that will fit any of the cabin doors on the *Persephone*. We keep all the cabin doors locked, and be sure to keep yours locked when you leave them. There's a regular plague of theft here in Alaska. And we'll do everything we can to make you as comfortable as possible while you're waiting to continue your trip."

"I'm sure that you will," Jessie agreed. The irritation triggered earlier by her discovery of the delay they were encountering was fading now.

Klaus had stood by silently during the exchange between Jessie and the purser. He walked beside Jessie and Ki when they stepped off the ship, and as they stopped on the shore outside to look along the waterfront and the zigzag trail that led to the beached ship, he rested his hand on Jessie's arm.

"If it is your concern that the time we must wait will to me be an inconvenience, Jessie, do not be perturbed," he said. "I will be glad to have a chance to see this cold, bare country. My father has told me a little about his experiences here, and from what he says I am sure that such a place as it is we do not have in any of the parts of Europe I have visited."

"I'm glad you feel that way, Klaus," she replied. "And I'm really not as angry as I might've sounded. We may just be able to put our waiting time to good use."

"Oh?" Klaus frowned. A puzzled expression was beginning to form on his face. "And how is that possible, when we are still so far from our destination?"

"After Ki and I had decided we'd make this trip, we went through Alex's old files," Jessie explained. "We found that among the dozen or more claims he staked here in Alaska there are three or four that he never did sell. If any of them are close by, I think I'd like to look at them."

"You are perhaps planning to sell these claims yourself, then?" Klaus asked.

"I haven't decided yet, Klaus," Jessie answered. "First of all, I'm not sure that anybody would want to buy them."

"From what I have heard on the ship while we traveled here, I would say you should have little trouble finding buyers," Klaus told her. "I believe many people like to gamble that such claims will prove to be very rich."

"Yes, gold seekers are the world's greatest gamblers." Ki nodded. "From what Jessie and I learned when we were going over Alex's old papers, he made a great deal of money buying and selling unproved claims."

"That's true," Jessie agreed. "But I couldn't find records that any of the claims Alex didn't sell have been proved. I don't know whether they're valuable or totally worthless."

"You know where they are, though?" Klaus asked.

"Not precisely, of course," Jessie replied. "But even though I wasn't sure we'd have time find out about them, I brought the claim maps along. Now that we've unexpectedly got some time to spare, we may be able to reach the ones that are reasonably close."

"There certainly isn't much to look at here," Ki said. "We don't have too much choice about what to do, except wait. I'd suggest the first thing we should do after we get settled into our new accommodations is to go to that store up the slope and buy some food. They'll probably be able to tell us where the nearest assay office is located. We'll have to go to one to find out exactly where those claims are located."

"And we'll get a map of the territory, if they have such

a thing," Jessie added. "From what little we've seen on our way up here, that's something we're going to need pretty badly."

Silently, their spirits a bit dampened by the unexpected delay they were encountering, they covered the short distance that remained to the beached steamship. The forequarter of the vessel's keel was buried in the soft, mucky riverbank, and a short gangway led to the forepeak, but it was surprisingly level. Jessie, Ki and Klaus went up the gangplank to the deck, then up the ladderlike stair that led to the upper decks, where the passenger cabins were located.

"I can't say that I like having to shift for ourselves, but I don't see that we have any choice," Jessie said as they stopped on the upper deck of the *Persephone* and looked along the row of cabin doors that lined the narrow passage around the deck, between the outer rail and the rise of the vessel's superstructure. She indicated the doors as she went on, "I suppose that if there are any other stranded passengers on board, they'll have locked their cabin doors. The easiest thing I can see for us to do is open each of the unlocked doors and look in until we find the locked one our luggage is in. I'm sure they've put us in adjoining cabins."

"It's as good a way as any," Ki agreed. "Suppose you and Klaus start on this side. I'll go to the other side."

"Yes, we'll finish a lot faster that way," Jessie agreed. She took one of the keys given her by the purser and handed it to Ki, saying, "This will open any of the cabin doors." Turning to Klaus, she handed him a key and suggested, "Why don't you go up and check the upper deck? This ship's like the *Nancy Belle*, there are only about half as many cabins up there. If Ki and I each check one side on this deck, we should all be finished at about the same time."

74

Klaus nodded and began moving toward the vessel's stern. Jessie stood in the prow for a moment, gazing at the mountain peaks that formed the jagged distant skyline. Though they were not spectacularly tall, even at this time in the middle of the short Alaskan summer they were still capped with snow.

With a shrug, Jessie turned and opened the door of the first cabin. It was bare, the bunks untouched. She moved to the next one, and found that it, too, was unoccupied. The third door was locked. Jessie fitted the key she'd kept into the lock and opened the door. Klaus's heavy leather suitcase stood in the middle of the floor. Stepping back outside, she looked along the narrow strip of deck. Klaus was nowhere visible. Moving to the rail, Jessie waited for him to show himself again.

Ki had moved rapidly along the walkway on the other side of the vessel. He opened each cabin door in turn, gave a quick glance around to be sure it was unoccupied before moving on to the next. By the time he'd gotten a bit more than halfway to the prow of the ship, he'd found two staterooms in which keys in the lock inside blocked his.

He reached the next door in the line, which still stretched ahead, and inserted his key. When the key met no resistance, he turned the knob and gave the door a soft push with his toe. It swung open, and the first thing that caught his notice was the tousled condition of the bedding in the lower berth.

Realizing that he'd opened one of the occupied staterooms, Ki took a half step backward and started to pull the door closed. It was just beginning to swing shut when the bedclothes stirred and heaved.

Before Ki could complete his turn the bedding dropped away to reveal a woman starting to sit up in the lower section of the bunk. She swiveled her torso as she leaned forward, bowing her head before it struck the bottom of the bunk above.

Ki's imperturbability vanished. He blinked with surprise as the woman dropped the bedding and he saw that she was naked. Her breasts swayed gently as she turned to look toward the opened doorway.

"Hello, lovey," she said, cocking her head sidewise as though to get a better look at him. "I don't know who it was that steered you to me, but now you've found me, come on in."

"I'm sorry," Ki said. "I didn't mean to intrude."

"Well, I sure ain't a bit sorry," she replied. "If you hadn't come along, I'd likely've slept on the whole damn day. Now you're here, just put the money in that saucer on the dressing table. No paper money, mind you. Ten cartwheels or a gold eagle, just like the usual. By the time you've got your breeches pulled down, I'll have these bedclothes pushed out of the way and be all ready for you."

"I—I'm sorry, but you've made a mistake," Ki said. "I wasn't looking for companionship. I'm trying to find the stateroom of a friend."

"You don't know how friendly I can be till you've tried me." As she spoke, the woman was pushing herself toward the edge of the bunk. She dropped her feet to the floor and sat with her shoulders slumped, her breasts dangling and undulating gently as she leaned forward to avoid the bottom of the upper bunk.

"Now, stop being bashful," she went on. "Come on over here where I can reach you. Seems like you might need a little extra attention before you can make up your mind."

"Thank you," Ki replied. "But I have some business that I must attend to. It's very urgent, so I'll bid you good day and let you finish resting."

Before she could reply, Ki backed out of the stateroom, closing the door behind him. He moved on along the row of doors, checking each of the rooms in turn without receiving any more surprises. When he'd reached the ship's prow and rounded the high-set wheelhouse, he saw Jessie standing in the open door of her cabin and hurried to join her.

"I've found our staterooms," she said as Ki came within easy speaking distance. "At least, I've found mine, and you and Klaus must be in the next two. I haven't gone beyond mine yet; I was just starting to look for you and Klaus to tell you that you needn't waste any more time."

"You didn't find any more passengers waiting over, I suppose?" Ki asked.

"No. Did you?"

"I found just one stateroom that I'm sure was occupied," Ki replied. "But the locks on two others that I tried had keys in their locks on the inside, so I suppose there are a few others aboard besides ourselves."

"They're probably waiting for the same ship we are," Jessie said. "But now that we're sure of having a place to sleep, we'd better be thinking about food. As soon as Klaus gets back, let's go ashore and see what we can find to eat while we're waiting."

As though mentioning his name had been a summons, Klaus appeared around the opened door where Jessie was standing. When he saw Jessie and Ki he said, "I have found nobody, but there are several doors that have been locked which I did not open."

"Then you found about the same thing that Ki and I did," Jessie told him. "And since there doesn't seem to be anything more that we can do here, suppose we get out our heavy coats, lock our cabins and go up to the store the purser told us about to see what we can find to eat during the time we'll be waiting."

After their long voyage from San Francisco, the feeling of solid ground underfoot was a welcome one as they started up the incline and headed for the nearest cluster of buildings. As they drew closer to the blocky, closely spaced structures it was easy to see that they not only were deserted, but that the desertion had taken place many years ago. The buildings were of yellow brick and had at one time been sturdy and strong. Now the bricks had fallen away from the once-square borders of windows and doors, creating ragged-edged holes that formed black blotches against the light-hued walls.

"Those buildings must have been very imposing in this wild, untamed country," Jessie commented. "I wonder why they've been left to fall to pieces."

"I can a guess make," Klaus volunteered. "My father has told me of the times he was here many years ago, before Alaska was by your country bought. To Russia it then belonged, and they had trading stations for the fine furs they prize so dearly. The furs were the property of the tsar himself, and only he could have ordered such huge buildings to be put up in a place so far from anywhere."

"That makes good sense," Jessie nodded. "But why would anyone leave—"

Her question was never completed. A spurt of red muzzle-

78

blast came from one of the pitch-black openings that had once been a window, and as the shot from the rifle broke the quiet air the angry buzz of a rifle bullet whistled as it cut the air above their heads.

★

Chapter 7

Jessie and Ki dropped flat just as the high-pitched wasp-like humming of the rifle slug broke the quiet air above their heads. Klaus stood staring ahead in frozen amazement for a moment, as though he was stunned by the sound of gunfire in a place that appeared to be so peaceful. When Jessie glanced up and saw that he was still on his feet, she moved quickly. Rolling to the spot where Klaus was still standing gazing at the buildings, she grabbed the hem of his greatcoat and tugged it urgently.

Klaus did not need a second warning to spur him into action. He dropped to join Jessie and Ki, stretching out on the ground beside them. For a moment the three lay prone and motionless, waiting for a second shot, but no more rifle fire came from the clustered buildings to shatter the quiet midafternoon air.

"Did you see which of those buildings that shot came

from, Ki?" Jessie asked after a moment had passed and their observation of the buildings showed no further sign of life.

"I wasn't watching them too closely, Jessie," Ki answered. "But I'm almost sure I saw a wisp of powder smoke coming from the one on our left."

"Who on earth would want to shoot us, Ki?" she went on. "It's been a long time since we were in Alaska, and we've never been in this part of it before."

"I don't think we could even guess who fired at us, Jessie," Ki said. "But I'm pretty sure they weren't trying to hit us."

"Just a warning?" Jessie frowned. "Telling us to stay away from the buildings?"

"If *der scheissener* to harm us intended, more than one bullet he would have fired," Klaus observed before Ki could reply.

"You're right, Klaus," Jessie agreed. "And since we don't have any reason for going into those buildings, or even closer to them than we are now, I suggest the best thing we can do is to make what in the army would be called a strategic retreat."

"A very good suggestion." Ki nodded. "But let's don't give them any chance to mistake what we're doing when we first move. If we stand up, whoever's inside there might think we intend to go toward the buildings instead of away from them, so let's do our turning around while we're still on the ground."

Jessie nodded her agreement. Then she suggested, "We'd better go one at a time instead of all three moving at once. If we did that, the sniper still might get a wrong idea about what we're planning to do. You go first, Klaus. Just turn around without standing up and belly-crawl until you've covered fifteen or twenty feet. Then stop and wait for Ki and me to catch up with you. We'll be just a little way behind you."

"It is you who must go first, Jessie," Klaus told her. "Let me and Ki the rear guard be."

At another time Jessie might have argued the question, but she recognized that their most urgent need was to convince the concealed sniper that they were going to retreat. "All right," she agreed. "I'll go first, but don't you and Ki wait too long to follow me."

Turning without rising from the ground, Jessie began crawling away from the still-silent buildings. Neither Ki nor Klaus changed position, but both of them swiveled their heads to watch her. When she'd covered fifteen or twenty feet and no shot sounded from the ruined buildings, Ki gestured to draw Klaus's attention.

"It's your turn now, Klaus," he said without taking his eyes from the buildings. "And you know what to do. I'll give you a little bit of a start, then I'll follow you."

Klaus nodded. He wormed around and began crawling as Jessie had. Ki watched for a moment or two before moving, then followed the example set by his companions. When he reached the place where Jessie and Klaus had stopped, he swiveled his head to look back at the decaying buildings.

There was still no sign of life from them, and he got to his feet, moving slowly. Jessie and Klaus followed his example. For a moment all three of them were busy dusting their clothing, then Jessie broke the silence.

"Has any idea occurred to either of you about who might've shot at us?" she asked.

Klaus and Ki shook their heads, and after a moment of silence Ki said slowly, "Wild country draws wild people,

Jessie. Standing alone as they do, those buildings have probably gotten to be a hideout or a shelter for any outlaws who might be traveling this way."

"In the homeland we have too few outlaws for me to know of their ways," Klaus said. "But what you have said seems likely, Ki. From the way they appear, the buildings have not been used for many years."

"That's my idea, too." Jessie nodded. "And I'm even more certain than before that those buildings were put up by the Russians. They're so big and well built that it's a shame to see them just falling apart."

"I imagine our government thought it was more important to attend to the little section of Alaska that's on the mainland than to spend their time on an isolated place like this," Ki suggested. "After the United States bought Alaska there'd've been a lot of work involved in getting the new border with Canada straightened out and replacing the Russian officials with people who're familiar with the way we do things."

"Well, that's not our worry at the moment," Jessie went on. "We'd better be spending our time getting some food and then settling into our new quarters. Let's just circle around the buildings and go on to that little settlement further up the slope to see what we can find in the way of food."

"That is what I, too, should like to do," Klaus put in. "Breakfast was a long while since, and I am beginning to be very hungry."

"We can probably find some cheese and soda crackers at the store up the slope there," Ki told them. "Maybe a few airtights, or something else that we can eat without having to cook. It's not likely that we'll have any sort of kitchen to use on that grounded ship."

"I'm sure we'll find enough food to keep us going for the few days we'll be here," Jessie said cheerfully as they started making their way up the slope. "At least, let's hope it's only going to be a few days."

By this time they were moving slowly up the slope, angling across its cracked and barren ground. The only vegetation in sight was a sort of mossy ground-hugging plant that grew in small, widely scattered patches. As they encountered a stand of the dark green growth, Ki turned to Jessie and pointed toward the short thin stalks.

"I wouldn't like to be grazing a herd of steers in this part of Alaska," he said. "It'd take a whole section of land just to keep one steer alive."

"Oh, Alaska's a big place, Ki," Jessie replied. "There must be some places where there's grassland and water and maybe even a few trees."

"And who would trade gold for cattles?" Klaus asked.

"It's done every day in the livestock exchanges," Jessie said quickly. "But in one sense of the word, Ki's right. This is mining country, not cattle range."

Although the slope they were ascending was fairly steep, while they talked they'd been making good progress over the hard soil, since reaching the winding trail that had been worn into the earth just below the peaks of the ridge. Though they'd been watching carefully, they'd seen no signs of life.

Now the first dwelling in the straggling line of small houses was just ahead. There were fewer than a dozen of them, and they had three things in common: no two were alike; except for the largest all were jerry-built; and none of them showed any signs that they were inhabited. While good lumber had gone into the construction of the larger

85

structures, the smaller ones were made of sod bricks and bits and pieces of boards in odd sizes held together precariously by lashings of rigging rope and rusted wire on foundations of native boulders.

In contrast to so many of the shanties, good lumber had gone into the the big building that stood at the far end of the ragged row and dominated the smaller structures. It was the only building that boasted a chimney, though no smoke was emerging from its top. It had a few windows, two or three of them paned with isinglass and the remainder with variously sized pieces of glass. Like the other dwellings in the short row, it appeared to be unoccupied.

"I certainly hope the purser on the *Nancy Belle* knew what he was talking about when he told us we'd find a store up here," Jessie said as they drew close to the building. "This building's big enough to be one, but it looks as deserted as the others."

"We'll soon know," Ki told her. "I've seen equally ramshackle little settlements in remote places in China, Jessie, and in the West you and I have both seen some pretty shabby houses in mining camps that were just getting started."

"Yes, I suppose you're right," Jessie agreed. "And as you said, it won't take us much longer to find out."

"We must first discover where is the door," Klaus said. "I can see only windows."

"It's probably on the south side of the building," Jessie told him, glancing up at the sun, which was now dropping down toward the horizon. "I'd imagine that the north wind gets pretty biting in the wintertime."

They were passing along the big building's walls as she spoke, and when they rounded the corner of the sprawling structure, they found her guess to be a good one. The south wall was broken by two windows and a double door. All three were closed, but when Ki stepped up to try the doorknob, it turned readily, and he pushed the door open.

Ki gestured for Jessie and Klaus to wait, then stepped inside, where he stood examining the big room he'd entered. It was a study in contradictions. One of the three ship's lamps that hung from the rafters was lighted, and by its yellowed gleam Ki glanced around. The interior managed to look barrenly cavernous and at the same time crowded.

A huge base burner stove dominated one corner. The stove stood some distance away from the walls in front of a stairway. At the foot of the stairs a gaggle of chairs, all sizes and configurations, were clustered seat to seat and arm to arm. They crowded the line of benches that ran along the wall. Some of the benches were elaborate church pews, some merely backless benches, but both benches and chairs bore the shine of long and regular use.

Tiers of shelves lined the walls, the regularity of their lines broken only by the windows. A good half of the shelves were bare, but those remaining were crowded with airtights and bundles wrapped in cloths that shined with grease; the varying formation of their bulges indicated that they held sausages and slabs of bacon or hams. Along one side wall bolts of cloth were stacked willy-nilly on the shelves. Ki gave these only a passing glance, then turned his full attention to scanning the room's cavernous interior.

Counters stood along the side walls in front of the shelves. No two of them were exactly alike; their width and height varied, and so did the hues of the wood from which they had been made. In front of the counters cracker-barrels protruded at irregular intervals. At the end of one of the counters a massive and badly scarred chopping block stood.

Its surface was as uneven as the low humped hills of the terrain outside. On it rested a cheese cutter, part of a slab of bacon and the shank of a ham.

Stepping back to the door, Ki motioned for Jessie and Klaus to join him. They came in and immediately were caught up, just as Ki had been, in an inspection of the store's interior.

After a single swift glance at the shelves behind the chopping block, Jessie said, "At least we won't starve while we're waiting, even if we have to get along for a few days on cheese and crackers."

"I'm sure there'll be something more than that," Ki said, indicating the shelves behind the block and the counter that extended beyond it to the stairs. "I'd imagine there'll be tomatoes and beans and turnips and such-like in those airtights."

Before Jessie had time to reply, thumps from the stairway drew their attention. They turned away from their examination of the store's interior to look at the man descending the stairs.

At first glance he appeared to be imposingly large, but as he reached the floor and started toward them, they were able to tell that he was short in stature and that his size was an illusion created by the thickly padded jacket he was wearing. His face was seamed and his skin so deeply tanned that at first they took him to be from one of the dark-skinned races. He walked in a jerking fashion, which they could now see was forced on him by a pegleg, though from the rapidity of his movements it seemed he'd learned long ago to adjust to it almost automatically.

"Come to rustle up some grub, I guess?" he asked. Then before any of the three could reply he went on, "I've heard some talk about that damn gussied-up steamboat you come on not going no further up the sound."

"That's right," Jessie agreed. "We're having to wait a few days for another ship to get here, so we'll need some food to carry us over."

"Likely I've got whatever it'll take to please you," he said, jerking a thumb toward the shelf where the greasy bundles were stowed. "Ham and bacon and sausages, and if you don't want meat there's plenty of cheese. Now, you just name what strikes your fancy. My meat and cheese is all the same price, ten dollars a pound. And I don't take paper money nor script, just good solid gold or silver."

Jessie had been expecting to pay a high price for their needs, for she and Ki had been in many boom towns where food was hard to come by and merchants boosted their prices accordingly. Though she had not been expecting the figure the storekeeper had quoted, she allowed no surprise to show in her voice but nodded and went on.

"Suppose you cut us two pounds of each kind of your ready-to-eat meat and another two pounds of cheese," she said. "We'll need bread or crackers to eat with the meat, and if you've got some cans of Mr. Borden's new-fangled preserved milk, we'll take one or two of them as well as some tea."

"I got plenty of ship biscuits," the man told her. "But if you're talking about milk put up like garden greens and such in airtights, that's something I ain't even heard about till now. I got more tea than I know what to do with, though. Cheap, too. I'll let you have the best Formosa oolong for just a dollar an ounce."

"That would be refreshing, Jessie," Ki broke in. "The tea he mentions is very fine indeed."

"We'll get a few ounces, then," Jessie said. "Can you think of anything I've missed, Ki?"

"Only one thing," he said. "Information."

"I haven't forgotten," she assured him. "I was hoping that Mr. . . . " She turned back to the proprietor and went on, "I'm sure you know that we're strangers here—"

"Sure," he broke in. "There's more damn cheechako around here now than there is us folks this place belongs to. If you don't catch on to what I mean by—"

"Cheechakos," Jessie broke in. "As it happens, I do know. I learned what it means from my father, who spent quite a bit of time in Alaska before his death. His name was Alex Starbuck."

"I've heard about him." The man nodded. There was a subtle change in his voice as he went on. "That was a pretty good bunch of years ago, when I was a cheechako myself. I never run into him, but I never heard nobody say nothing but good about him. Which ain't going to make no differences when we're doing business, I might say."

"Yes. I can understand that," Jessie went on. "But we're new to Alaska, and we depend on you folks who live here to tell us many of the things we need to know to get along."

"What's got you curious?" the storekeeper asked.

"Quite a number of things, Mr. . . . " Jessie paused and a small frown flicked across her face as she went on, "I'm sorry, but I didn't catch your name."

"Schwatka's the name I been traveling under ever since I made up my mind to stay here, even if I had to jump ship to do it," he told her. "And that was a long time ago. I wouldn't tell my right name to nobody, not even Alex Starbuck's girl. What few friends I got hereabouts just call me Swat."

90

Jessie nodded and went on, "We started to look at those big buildings down by the shore, and even before we got very close to them, somebody inside one of them started shooting at us."

"I ain't surprised," Schwatka said. "It couldn't've been nobody but one of them Russkies that deserted from their army and stayed behind when they pulled out."

"But that was years and years ago," Jessie frowned. "Surely there couldn't be many Russians left by now."

"Well, there was something like thirty or forty that didn't want to go home," he replied. "Most of 'em drifted away, started trapping or set up as guides. Some of 'em turned outlaw, and they're the ones you better look out for. There's a few of 'em in that little gang of renegades that's nested up in those old buildings."

"Then it had to be one of them shooting at us." Jessie frowned. "But we hadn't done anything to make them feel that we were threatening them."

"You didn't even need to act like you was going to go inside of one of them buildings," Schwatka told her. "All you had to do was be close to 'em. Letting off a shot's their way of telling folks that visitors ain't welcome. Now, let me get busy and get your order together."

"We'll just give them a wide berth, then," Ki said as he and Jessie followed the storekeeper to the counter.

"We shouldn't be here long enough to be in any danger from them," Jessie added. "But we'll keep our eyes open."

"And keep your six-gun handy, too," Schwatka advised without turning away from the shelves, where he was taking down some of the bundles.

He moved swiftly, with the economical motions of a

person doing a familiar job, as he cut slices of meat and placed them on the scale, where he'd spread a length of tattered cloth to serve as a wrapper. While he was working, with Jessie and Ki watching, Klaus had begun moving slowly around the store's interior, examining the items on its shelves.

He reached a pair of low tables in one corner that held a scattered miscellaneous mixture of items that appeared to be preponderantly bits and pieces of used personal property. Since they were already in disarray, he began poking into the small heaps, and, after finding nothing that was either interesting or useful, was about to turn away when, near the bottom of a heap of half-toothless combs and tattered remnants of ragged, faded bandanas and torn gold-dust pokes and split wooden handles of razors without blades, the gleam of what appeared to be ivory caught his eye.

Idly, Klaus pushed away the detritus that covered the yellowed ivory and pulled it free. He saw at once that it was the frame and handle of a clasp knife that lacked a blade. He was about to toss it back on the table when he saw that the handle had an inset oval of silver that bore an inscription. Still only half-interested, he lifted it to read the lettering. His eyes opened and his interest in the broken knife suddenly boiled up when he read the engraved letters: A. STARBUCK.

"Jessie!" Klaus called, trying to keep his voice from showing the excitement he felt. "For a moment, please come here. I have found something which I am sure will be of interest to you."

★

Chapter 8

"What is it that you've found, Klaus?" Jessie asked as she turned away from the counter and started toward him.

"I have found something which I should like to give you," Klaus replied. "Something I believe you will be both surprised and delighted to see."

As Jessie reached Klaus's side he handed her the knife, being careful to place it on the palm of her extended hand with the side containing the inscription on the bottom. A small, puzzled frown formed on her face as she looked down for a moment at the little, elongated ivory knife-hasp. Then she said, "I don't understand why you think I'd be at all interested in a pocketknife. Especially one that doesn't even have a blade."

"On the other side you might look," Klaus suggested.

Half-closing her hand to turn the knife over, Jessie glanced at it cursorily. She saw the small silver plate with its engraved inscription, but with the knife held almost at waist-level she could not make out the lettering until she'd raised her hand higher. For a moment Jessie could do nothing but stare unbelievingly, then her eyes widened and her jaw dropped.

"How on earth did you separate this from all the junk that's on the table?" she asked.

"Almost I did not, Jessie," he replied. "I saw first the small gleam of ivory and thought it might be engraved and that when to the homeland I return I might take it as a small souvenir. I was surprised very greatly to see your father's name, but at once I knew that you must have it."

"You know I appreciate it, Klaus," Jessie said. "And I'll thank you more adequately when we're alone. But I wonder if the storekeeper remembers how he got this." She stepped back to the counter, where Schwatka was wrapping their purchases in a somewhat tattered piece of thick brown paper. Holding out the knife, she asked, "Do you know how this knife came to be on your little table over there?"

"That's where I keep the junk stuff the natives come in to swap," he replied. He took the knife to examine it more closely, and when he saw the engraved plate his face brightened. "Sure," he went on. "This has been on the junk table for such a long time I'd forgot all about it, and didn't even remember till right now that it's got your daddy's name on it. I swapped for it—oh, it'd be all of fifteen years back, maybe twenty. Some Aleut brung it in. I figured I'd put a new blade in it, but it turned out to be too big of a job, so I just tossed it in with the junk on that table."

"I wish please to buy it," Klaus said quickly. "So that Miss Starbuck may own it. What is your price?"

A momentary frown rippled across Schwatka's face, vanishing even before it was fully formed. He shrugged and said, "It ain't worth dickering over." Turning away from Klaus to face Jessie, he handed her the knife as he went on, "You and your friends has done a right good piece of business with me, Miss Starbuck. Suppose I just throw in the knife for boot."

"But I wish the knife to be my gift," Klaus protested. "I will be glad to pay—"

Jessie broke in, "I'll always remember that you're the one who found it, Klaus, and that's what's important. You know how I'll treasure it. But let's settle up now with Mr. Schwatka and go on back to the ship. I hate to be away from it too long, because we don't have even the ghost of an idea when we might be called to continue our trip. We'd better be ready to leave on very short notice."

"If we're forced to stay here very long, we'll need to make another trip to Schwatka's store," Ki said to Jessie as they wrapped up the remnants of their food that evening after their picnic meal in her cabin. "We ate a great deal more than I had thought we would."

"It's easy enough to go back to the store," Jessie replied. "But before we do, I intend to make some very strong suggestions to whoever's in charge of the steamship line."

"Suggestions?" Ki frowned.

"Yes. That it's their responsibility to feed us," she replied.

"This perhaps we should have done when we were told that we must wait here," Klaus suggested.

"Being told about it was a surprise to me," Jessie admitted. "It didn't occur to me that our trip might be interrupted, or that we might have to stay in such an isolated place for any length of time. I suppose I should have. But we have enough food to carry us through another day or so. Let's just hope that the boat we're having to wait for will be here soon."

"And in the meantime, we may as well rest," Ki suggested. "It's been a very busy day, and I don't mind admitting that I'll be glad to stretch out on my bunk." He stood up and stretched, then went on, "I'm sure you and Klaus must feel the same way, Jessie, so I'm going to say good night now and go to bed."

"I feel a bit sleepy," Klaus said. Then he gestured toward the porthole set into the outer wall, where bright rays of sunlight were still streaming in despite the late hour, as he went on, "But going to bed by daylight is a thing to which I have not yet grown accustomed."

"I suppose we'll all need a little time to get used to it," Jessie said. "I suppose we just didn't realize until we got this far north that Alaska really is the land of the midnight sun."

"Instead of trying to get used to it, do as your father told me that he did when he first came to Alaska," Ki advised. "He learned to hang a dark-colored cloth over his shack's windows, and it would be just as effective in here over the porthole. I've tried it, and it works. It won't make your stateroom dark in the manner night does, but it will turn down the glow of what Alaskans call the midnight sun."

To the accompaniment of good nights from his companions, Ki went out into the chill that a freshly borne breeze was carrying across the water to the vessel. In spite of the penetrating chill, he did not hurry to his stateroom but stopped beside the rail for a moment, looking over the dancing reflection of the bright sunshine reflected on the surface of the inlet's water. Then the cold air began to seep through the fabric of his loose blouse and trousers, and he moved on to his stateroom.

Although Ki had been sure that he'd locked the door of the little cubicle, his key met no resistance when he inserted it into the lock and turned it; nor was there any rasping from a bolt. Telling himself that he'd been lax in forgetting to lock the door before joining Jessie and Klaus earlier in the day, Ki stepped inside and closed the door. Then in the gloom he ran his fingertips along its jamb to find the night latch that he remembered having seen during his earlier and very brief stay.

As the bolt clicked home, he turned away, relaxing while waiting for his eyes to adjust to the dimness of the room. His relaxation was brief. Ki's muscles tightened involuntarily when from the bunk on the opposite wall of the cramped stateroom a woman's voice broke the silence.

"I was wondering how much longer I'd have to wait for you, dearie," she said. "Seems to me I've been here a long time."

Ki recovered from his surprise almost instantly and said quickly, "Perhaps you'd better tell me who you are and what you're doing in my stateroom."

"Just call me Winnie," she replied. "And you'd oughta be able to figure out that I come here to wait for you, like I just said. Except when I come in here I didn't expect you to be gone for such a long time."

"You—you must be the lady I saw this morning," Ki said as the memory of the stateroom that he'd entered by mistake, while making his quick preliminary inspection of the ship, flashed into his mind.

"I sorta thought you'd remember," she nodded. "You see, I don't do like a lot of us girls. I ain't too stuck up to go

97

looking for a man when I need one, instead of waiting for him to come and look for me."

Ki's eyes had adjusted to the gloomy dusk of the little cubicle by now, and he could see her outlined against the white bedclothes. In the dim light he could make out only a few details. He got the suggestion that her eyes were dark and her lips red and full. The remainder of her face was a white blur.

Her body stood out against the shaded wall behind the bunk, an outline of shoulders and arms. The dark twin circles of her pebbled bosom spots only accented their protruding tips and the lighter shadows that revealed her breasts' full bulges, just as the darkly blurred triangle of her pubic bush emphasized and drew his eyes away from the arch of her swelling thighs.

"I'm a bit curious about how you managed to get in," Ki told her.

"Why, one key fits all these cabin door locks," she answered. "That's the first thing us girls learns when we start working ships."

"So you had no trouble opening the door when you decided to come and—as you just said—work me."

Winnie was silent for a moment, then she said, "I didn't mean it the way it sounded."

When Ki did not reply, she fell silent, as did Ki. Then, just as the quiet that had taken over the little cabin became a strain, she spoke again.

"I got a hunch you're one of the decent kind," she said, speaking slowly and thoughtfully. "And I've known enough men to be able to tell a lot about one real quick. So let me tell you something that I likely wouldn't say to anybody else. After a girl's bedded twenty or thirty men a night for three or four years, she gets so used to having somebody prodding her that she misses it something fierce when a man don't come her way regular. And she don't look to see whether whoever's giving it to her is white or black or yellow or brown."

"Then that's why you came looking for me?" Ki asked. "For your own satisfaction, not for money?"

"Oh, I won't turn money down," Winnie replied. "But if you don't have any, that don't mean I'm going to walk away, till this itch between my legs gets eased. Now, I don't guess I can put it to you much plainer."

"No, I don't suppose you can," Ki agreed.

He spoke slowly. He could see Winnie's nude body clearly now, and suddenly he become aware that seeing her, combined with the frank expression of her desires, was bringing him to an erection. Though Ki knew that he could control his urges, he had no desire to do so. After the long period of continence he'd undergone during the time he'd spent in the isolation of the Circle Star, he realized only too well that he was ready to welcome the woman's visit.

"Well, how about it?" Winnie asked when several moments had passed and Ki said nothing more.

Ki did not reply with words but tugged at the knot of the narrow sash that held the front of his loose jacket together. Winnie leaned forward to help him remove it. The brushing together of their warm hands, as they met while freeing the sash, increased Ki's urgency. By this time he had no intention of drawing away. He shrugged out of the jacket and let it fall to the floor.

Winnie reached out to him at once and began to unbutton the waistband that served Ki as a belt. It was obvious that she neither needed nor wanted help, for each time that she freed one of the buttons of his waistband, she'd lift her hand to brush it in a soft caress over the sleek, rippling muscles of his biceps and chest.

When Ki's loose trousers slid to the floor, she ran her hand searchingly over his bulging crotch, but the folds of his *cache-sex* defeated her. She fumbled in her search without success until at last Ki reached for the tucked-away end of the wide strip of white linen and pulled it free. The encircling layers of closely woven fabric cascaded down his thighs and calves to the floor, and from that point on Winnie wasted no time.

While the end of the cloth was still crumpling onto the floor, she threw an arm around Ki's shoulders to lever herself upward. Her legs went around his hips, and her free hand slid between their close-pressed bodies until she could grasp his erection and place the swollen shaft.

Ki felt her heels drumming on his buttocks the instant that she'd accomplished her purpose, and then Winnie jerked her shoulders backward and tightened the embrace of her legs to pull him into her. She gasped when she felt him filling her, then threw herself backward onto the bunk, and Ki completed his penetration with a quick downward thrust as they landed on the mattress.

A hoarsely gargling moan of pleasure trickled from deep in her throat and was followed by a ululating sigh of satisfaction. Her voice hoarse with urgency, Winnie said, "Now, drive! And don't stop, not even if I beg you to!"

Ki obeyed her urgent plea. He started thrusting deeply in a slow, deliberate rhythm, pressing himself firmly against her body for a moment or two at the apex of each stroke. Winnie did not respond at once. She relaxed all her muscles and gave herself to Ki's measured lunges, content to lie motionless while passively accepting his slow rhythmic drives.

Ki did not hurry or increase the tempo of his thrusts until he felt Winnie beginning to twitch sharply at the completion of each penetration. Then he speeded up, but only very slightly. Even the small change in his tempo soon made Winnie's involuntary responses become more vigorous. She began bucking upward with greater gusto, and now Ki heard a sharper note starting to creep into the faint gasps she'd begun to loosen as he reached the end of each stroke.

Still Ki maintained the slow tempo of his drives, until at last Winnie's gasps became moans. The moaning was faint when it first began to replace her deep, gasping inhalations, but as Ki continued sinking into her deeply at the same measured pace, her moans grew louder. Ki speeded his stroking almost imperceptibly, and Winnie responded by matching it.

Now she was not contented merely to accept his steady lunges. She began to twist her hips while he was driving into her, and the slow tempo of her breathing broke the silence of the stateroom as each moment ticked away. When Ki started thrusting harder and at a faster pace, Winnie began an involuntary twitching as each of his thrusts ended. Ki felt the twitches and speeded up a bit more.

After the first moments of Ki's deeper and more vigorous thrusting, Winnie began whimpering. Her soft moans mounted steadily in both length and volume when Ki again increased the tempo of his stroking. Both of them were beginning to tremble now, and their stertorous sighs broke the hitherto still air of the dark cabin. Suddenly Winnie cried out, and at the same time she began to tremble in quivering undulations.

Ki read her signs. He began driving faster and even more vigorously, while Winnie writhed and the volume as well as the intensity of her cries grew greater. When she bucked and jerked and the trembling that was sweeping through her body became spastic and broken, Ki knew that her climax was beginning.

He drove fiercely now, thrust after lusty thrust until Winnie cried out in a hoarse, throaty yell and her hips heaved upward as her body began shaking. Ki relaxed the stern control he'd maintained for so many long minutes. He let his body take over until his urgency mounted and Winnie's cries peaked in a final shivering shriek, her back arched as she started to tremble uncontrollably.

At last Ki released himself completely and shivered as he jetted. His body jerked while Winnie's final spasms shuddered and faded. Then as she lay motionless except for the heaving of her bosom as she gasped for breath, he fell forward and lay limp.

Ki's chest was heaving, too. After he'd remained still long enough to regain the regular tempo of his breathing, he rolled away to lie pressed beside her on the narrow bunk. Now the only noise in the darkness of the cabin was the faint whistling of their breathing. For a short while they lay motionless, then a clatter of booted feet sounded on the deck outside.

Ki swung his legs over the edge of the bunk and sat up, then began fumbling on the floor to find his clothing. He picked up the first garment his fingers encountered and began pulling the fabric through his free hand to identify it. He discovered that he'd picked up his trousers and stood to step into them, for on the deck outside the clunking footsteps were growing steadily louder.

Winnie stirred in the bunk and asked sleepily, "You ain't going to leave me in here by myself, are you? Or send me back to my own cabin?"

"Of course not," Ki assured her. "But there's someone outside, and I think it would be much better if I go out to see who it is instead of waiting for them to come in here."

"And you'll be back?"

"Of course I will," Ki replied. "Just as soon as I make sure that we're not being visited by a burglar or some other kind of outlaw."

"That's all I wanted to know." She sighed as she stretched out and closed her eyes.

Ki did not wait to find any more of his garments. He finished donning his trousers and stepped into his sandals. Just as he opened the cabin door he heard footsteps close by. One quick step took him to the deck, and as he closed the door he saw the bulky figure of a man only two or three steps away. The man was moving closer to him, and now Ki could see that he had on the rough denims that were the common garb of waterfront workers.

"Are you looking for somebody?" he asked the newcomer.

"I sure as hell am. Three somebodies, as a matter of fact. One's a Miss Jessica Starbuck; then there's a fellow named Reiden and another one that's called Ki, so I guess he's some sort of chink. They said back at the pier that all of 'em are aboard here, but they told me not to give this envelope to nobody but Miss Starbuck."

"I am the some sort of chink," Ki said calmly, refusing to let the man's slurring phrase disturb him. "And I'm sure that Miss Starbuck is in her cabin, and Mr. Reiden in his. Both of them are on the other side of the ship. Would you like for me to show you which cabin Miss Starbuck is in?"

"I sure would. I got a message for her and you and this other fellow. It'll save me trying every damn cabin door on this tub looking for her, and you'll be handy, too."

"Then follow me," Ki said, pushing past the visitor to lead the way.

He led the new arrival to Jessie's cabin, and before the man could push ahead of him and knock, Ki tapped lightly on the door with his fingertips in a rhythm that both he and Jessie used to signal their identity to each other. After a momentary wait, Jessie called from within the cabin.

"Ki? Is something wrong?"

"Nothing at all, Jessie," he called back. "There's a man from the shipping line out here with a message for us, and I'm sure it won't take you any longer than it did me to figure out what it must be."

A moment later, the door of the cabin opened and Jessie stepped out. She was wearing a dressing gown and her hair was touseled. She blinked in the outdoor light and brushed some stray strands of blond tresses away from her forehead as she looked from Ki to the stranger.

"I'm Jessica Starbuck," she said.

"I figured you was," the man replied. "The boss told me to give this to you and not to nobody else."

As he spoke, the man handed Jessie an envelope. She opened it and took out a folded sheet of paper, which she unfolded and read at a glance. Then she turned to Ki and said, "Perhaps this midnight sunshine is a blessing in disguise. The ship we're waiting for to take us down the estuary and up the inward passage seems to have gotten here sooner than anyone expected. It'll be sailing in two hours. We'll have to hurry to get aboard."

★

Chapter 9

"Until I'd studied Alex's map for a while, I didn't really realize just how much extra traveling we'd have to do because of that mistake the steamship company made," Jessie told her companions.

"Let's just be glad the problem's cured and we know that we're heading for the right place at last," Ki said.

Jessie was standing between Ki and Klaus at the side rail of the *Sequoia*, the coastal-trade stern-wheel steamship they'd boarded four days earlier. They were enjoying their freedom to move around in spite of the nippingly fresh breeze coming off the water. During the first three days of the voyage a heavy fog had shrouded the water's surface, and the ship's captain had requested that all passengers stay in their cabins and keep out of the way of the crewmen while the vessel threaded through the tricky and treacherous Shelikof Strait.

After creeping at a snail's pace for what seemed to be an eternity, they'd passed through the strait into the Unimak Pass, which led to the Bering Sea. As the *Sequoia*'s bow swung northward after reaching open water, they found that they'd left the fog ashore. The dense grayish mist still obscured the land on the vessel's starboard side, but only a light veiling haze filtered the blue of the sky, and just above the water's surface the air was almost clear.

From their present position, the view beyond the vessel's prow was often blocked by the ship's wheelhouse, which jutted upward in a wide crescent above the deck. However, most of the time Jessie and her companions could see the shore below the fog on the vessel's right-hand side as the *Sequoia* chugged along. And the fog was dissipating rapidly. In some stretches it was high enough above the water's surface to reveal a strip of sky and the green foliage of the spruce and cedar trees that grew thickly on the rising ground beyond.

Jessie went on. "If we'd just had the proper booking in San Francisco instead of the substitutes we've been forced to accept, we'd have sailed from San Francisco right up the coast to Nome. As it is, we're having to backtrack and put in an extra week of traveling."

"It could have been much worse," Ki reminded her. "And I admit that since we first started out I've enjoyed the change of being on a ship at sea instead of in the saddle of a horse on the prairie."

"Or on a rattling train where the air's stale and you're confined in a single seat for hour after hour," Jessie added. The new tone in her voice told Ki that she'd uttered her last complaint and was accepting their situation with her usual grace. She went on, "Even as cold as it is here, we can

106

walk around the deck and breathe the fresh salt air."

"This also I enjoy," Klaus told them. "At home each day in an office chair I sit, and keep busy my head with turning francs and pounds and lira and dollars into deutsche marks, or around the other way. It is always the same. Here, each day is new and different."

"Yes." Jessie nodded. "At least this clumsy old stern-wheeler is moving, even if we haven't had much to look at besides the water, with an occasional glimpse of land through mist or fog."

"I would be satisfied if only we could be certain that the fog will some day soon vanish completely," Klaus said. "The land itself I should like to see. So much about Alaska I have from my father heard that I have the great curiosity."

"You'll see enough of Alaska to satisfy you, once we pass Nome," Jessie assured him. "If the maps we have are correct—and I'm sure they are, because Alex was very careful about everything he did—we'll need to travel quite a way inland to reach the claim."

"Yes, and we'll be lucky if we get to it and finish the job we've come to do before the real winter sets in," Ki said.

"I hope so," Jessie went on. "I don't think I'd like to be snowbound in the sort of wild country we've seen so far. But at least we'll be able to go on horseback. From what little Alex wrote in his diaries about prospecting inland from Nome, I've gotten a pretty good idea that we're getting started early enough to keep from having to use dogsleds."

"I have heard my father talk of using the sleds pulled by dogs," Klaus nodded. "And I do not think it is a kind of travel I should enjoy."

"There's one thing in my mind now," Jessie said. "It's getting—"

She did not get to finish what she'd started to reveal. A piercing, high-pitched laugh, the thin chortle of an excited child, broke the air. Cutting her words short, Jessie turned to look for the source of the laughter. Ki and Klaus joined her in swiveling around to look.

They saw a young boy, perhaps four or five years old, running toward them. He wore the universal garb of Alaska: butternut jeans and jacket and a railroad blue work shirt. A short distance behind him, just emerging from the stairway that connected the upper and lower decks, a woman was following him.

"Be careful, now, Jackie!" she called. "Remember what I told you, and don't go close to the railing!"

If the boy heard her, he gave no evidence of it; nor did he obey her command. He kept running toward the railing, which was a makeshift affair at best, a sturdy ship's cable that ran through waist-high eyebolts installed vertically around the perimeter of the deck. Only a few inches of deck extended beyond the point where the eyebolts were fixed to the decking.

At the head of the stairway the woman raised her voice again. "Jackie! Stop! Wait for me before you go any further!"

Her command was both urgent and needed, but it was also badly timed, for the boy was now less than a dozen feet from the cable. He turned at the sound of her voice but did not obey her order to stop. As he was swiveling in his turn his feet slipped and he fell. The momentum of his fall started him on a slide along the slanting deck toward its edge.

Before Jessie or Ki or Klaus had time to move, the boy's head bumped into the shaft of one of the eyebolts that supported the cable. Had the ship not wheeled in that critical moment, the boy would have been safe. The vessel was still canting, and though the youngster's arms flailed as he tried to grab the cable or its supporting shaft, the sharp angle the deck still maintained defeated him.

In a flurry of thrashing arms and legs the boy rolled on across the half-dozen inches that remained between him and the deck's rim. Within seconds his rolling course took him to the edge. Though the boy now saw his danger and began scrabbling wildly, trying to climb up the slick surface of the slanting deck, his efforts were futile.

None of the eyebolts supporting the cable were within his reach. He slid under the strand of cable to the edge of the deck and with a wailing scream dropped out of sight. Even before the child had fallen, Jessie and her companions had started moving toward him. They reached the spot where the boy had disappeared and looked over the cable that served as a rail.

For several moments that seemed to last an eternity they scanned the roiled surface of the dark froth-pocked wavelets until at last Ki spotted the black dot that was the youth's head. The slipstream of water flowing along the hull from the bow was already carrying the boy farther away from the vessel's side.

"There!" Jessie exclaimed, pointing. "That's him! Keep him in sight. I'm going to the pilothouse and have them stop the ship."

"We cannot help the boy in the water as long as we can only see him, Ki," Klaus said as Jessie started toward the prow. "And how are we to rescue him, now that we have located him?"

"He's a small boy," Ki replied. While he spoke, he was stepping out of his sandals. "And there's no need for both of us to jump overboard. You and Jessie get the ship stopped and find a long rope. I'll go after him."

"Wait, Ki!" Klaus protested. "Let me a cork ring find, to throw to you after you are in the water! On this ship there must be some! In that cold water your muscles quickly will grow stiff!"

"I'll be all right," Ki assured him. "But get the life rings; they might be needed later. Then come back here and stand by the rail so you can point to wherever the boy is by that time. I'll be watching for your signals."

Ki dived and was arrowing through the air before Klaus could say anything more. Klaus saw him hit the broad bow wave with a splash. The youngster had already been swept almost to the ship's stern. His head made a small lonely black dot amid the white froth on the water's roiled surface.

Turning, Klaus started running toward the pilothouse. Even before he reached the glassed-in structure, he could hear Jessie's voice.

" . . . but you must stop the ship now!" she was saying.

"Soon as I make sure you're right, ma'am. Them's orders," one of the two men in the glassed structure replied.

"Forget your—" she began before she saw Klaus. Then she turned to him and asked, "Do you know how to stop this ship, Klaus? These men aren't doing anything!"

"Ki has already jumped in to help the boy," Klaus told her. "But the ship we do not wish to stop. It must be turned swiftly, before we are too far away from them to help."

"I think the lady's right, Joe," the wheelman said, "And she'll likely help us square things up with Captain Baker."

Jessie took her cue from the wheelman's remark. She slid her Colt from her purse and levelled it at them as she said, "If you don't turn this boat around right now, I'll shoot you and take the wheel myself!"

Jessie's tone of voice and the muzzle of her Colt only inches from his face resolved any doubts in the wheelman's mind. He hesitated only a few seconds before he nodded and began to turn the big spoke-handles on the head-high wheel. Slowly, the vessel began to turn.

Ki's body hurtling downward broke the water's ripples with a splash. He kicked hard to bring himself to the surface, and as his head rose above the water, he glanced quickly at the vessel's towering bulk to orient himself. Then he started swimming, helped by the side stream created by the ship, trying to gauge direction and distance at the same time. Now and then he broke his strokes to kick hard against the tugging current created by the vessel's wake, and the kicks raised him high enough in the water to scan its frothed surface.

His first three or four efforts showed him nothing; then when he kicked with extra vigor, trying to lift his head even higher, the white froth on the surface gave him the help its dark undercurrents were working to deny him. Outlined against a wide streak of white froth a dozen yards away he saw the dark blob he'd been looking for, the boy's head showing as a quickly glimpsed bobbing sphere.

Now the seldom-used swimming skills, which Ki had acquired during countless water crossings in his home islands, returned to help him. He struck out for the floundering boy in strong sure strokes that propelled him rapidly through the icy foam-topped water.

111

Now and then Ki reared back while kicking vigorously to raise his head as high as possible above the surface. He did not see the boy's head each time he rose, but it was visible often enough to keep him moving steadily toward his goal. The slipstream created by the vessel was his friend now, sweeping him toward the youth, and Ki gauged his direction carefully. Although it seemed to him that he'd been in the bone-chilling water for hours, only a few minutes passed before he reached the side of the floundering boy.

"You're all right now," Ki said as his outstretched hand closed on the fabric of the youth's shirt. "Just keep still. Don't try to swim or move or do anything at all. I won't let you sink, and help's on the way."

When the *Sequoia* began to turn in response to the steersman's moves, the second crewman in the wheelhouse said to Jessie, "Lady, I don't know who who you are, but you're sure going to be in a heap of trouble soon as Captain Baker tumbles to what's going on in here."

"We'll worry about that when the captain arrives," Jessie told him. She did not raise her voice, but its authoritative tone carried its own message. "And he ought to be here right now, so suppose you go find him and tell him that two of his passengers need to be rescued from the water."

"There's no need to go looking for me," a new voice spoke from the narrow door at the end of the wheelhouse. "Now, one of you men tell me what this is all about."

Without taking her eyes off the men she was holding at gunpoint and before either of them had a chance to obey him, Jessie said, "You've got a passenger overboard and a man in the water out there trying to save him. We're getting farther away from them every minute."

112

"You better not be stretching the truth, lady," the captain said. His words carried an overtone of doubt. "But I'm not about to take any chances." Turning to the pilot, he went on, "Do what the lady says, Joe. Put about."

When the ship began to change its course as the helmsman slowly spun the big spoked wheel, Jessie relaxed. She returned her Colt to its holster and said, "My name's Jessica Starbuck, Captain. If you've looked at the passenger list—"

"I always do that," he replied. "You and two men with you are traveling to Nome. Now, what about this man overboard alarm?"

Jessie replied quickly, "To be as brief as possible, a young boy fell overboard and one of the men traveling with me dived in, trying to rescue him. They're well back of the ship now, closer to the shore. I'm sure you know how cold that water is, and we can't waste any time getting them out."

For a moment the captain stood silently staring at Jessie. Then he said, "Nobody's going to make up a yarn like that. But now that I'm here to take charge, I don't reckon we'll need your help any longer."

"I'm not at all interested in running your ship," Jessie assured him. "And I suppose you'll have some ideas about how to get them back on board here?"

"It's not as hard as you might think," he assured her. "We ought to be able to spot 'em right off. Soon as we do, I'll put a man on the main deck to stand by and throw them a line. Once they get hold of it, we'll haul them out." Turning to the two crewmen, he went on, "Joe, throttle down soon as we've finished putting about. Ed, you get out there on the forepeak and be ready to toss the line. I'll send a couple of deckhands forward to stand by on the cabin deck to grab them and help get them back on board."

"Klaus and I will go with you," Jessie said quickly. "We won't get in your way, but I intend to make sure that everything possible is being done."

"Don't worry, ma'am," Baker responded. "I've saved a lot more cheechakos than these two. Just you keep out from underfoot, and we'll have 'em back on board safe and sound inside of the next few minutes."

With Jessie close behind him, Captain Baker started for the deck. The ship was turning slowly, but steadily. The captain stepped to the rail and stopped, but Jessie hurried to join Klaus, who still stood close to the center of the ship, his eyes fixed on the water's surface.

"Are Ki and the boy safe?" she asked, holding her voice level and concealing her anxiety.

"They still keep above the water their heads," he replied. "To see them well is harder since we so far from them have gone, but they must I think now be swimming."

As Klaus spoke, he was pointing to the water's surface in a spot between the ship and the shore. Jessie scanned the area to which he was pointing and quickly spotted the two bobbing heads. At the sight of them, she was both surprised and alarmed when she saw how far the vessel had traveled since Ki dived into the water. Though the heads of the pair looked no larger than the tip of her thumb, her spirits lifted now that she realized they were still managing to keep afloat.

"We seem to be moving faster now," she said. "We'll soon be close enough for the crew to throw them a rope."

"When we do so, it will be for both of us a happy time," Klaus said. "I have come to respect your friend Ki very much indeed. It would grieve me if he should come to harm."

Jessie began scanning the water's surface toward the shore, looking for a stretch that was calmer than the area where Ki and the boy were, a place where getting them aboard would be easier. Some distance across a stretch of tumbled water and closer to the shore she saw a stretch of placid water and was examining it when Captain Baker spoke.

"If you've lost sight of your friends, they're a bit further from shore now and closer to us," he said. "Just look where I point and you'll see they're both still all right."

"I've already seen them, Captain," she replied. "I was looking for a place where it might be easier to help them get back on board. Like the calm stretch of water over beside the place where that big black hump of rock is sticking up."

Baker's eyes followed Jessie's pointing finger. His jaw dropped and he gulped, then gasped, "Oh, my God! That's not a rock you're looking at! That's a Greenland whaleshark, Miss Starbuck! It's damned near the size of a regular whale, and it's got a mouth and a set of teeth that'll bite through anything except chilled steel! And it eats anything that's moving!"

"Do you carry a rifle in your pilothouse?" Jessie asked.

"Sure," Baker replied. "But unless you hit that damned shark square in one of its eyes, you're wasting bullets."

"Please don't waste time!" Jessie exclaimed. "Just get the rifle for me, quickly!" Turning to Klaus, she went on, "And Klaus, hurry to my cabin and get my own rifle. I don't know how much time we have, but I'm not going to stand here looking on and do nothing to save Ki and the boy."

There was an authority in Jessie's tone that sent both the captain and Klaus on the errands she'd given them. Captain Baker returned first with the rifle from the pilothouse.

Wordlessly, he handed her the weapon. Jessie glanced at it, taking her eyes off the rounded black hump of the shark's back for the first time. The weapon was an old one, and she saw at a glance that she needed the power and penetration of her own weapon.

Jessie had been studying the dome of the Greenland whale-shark's back and comparing it with the size of a steer. She realized almost at once that the shark was equal in size to three or perhaps four steers pressed together and for a moment wished she had a Spencer buffalo gun.

"This is the first time I've ever heard of a Greenland whale-shark," Jessie said. Her voice was completely calm. "How much do you know about it?"

"Not much, except it can bite a man in two and swallow him in a minute or so. It's got a brain no bigger than my fist and it's one of the hardest fish in the ocean to kill," he replied. "I saw one take thirty shots one time and it was still going strong."

"Do you know where its brain is?"

"Right at the end of its jaws, where its back starts to slant up. But you're not going to try to—"

"Indeed I am," Jessie broke in. "If I can't kill it, I might be able to cripple it or drive it off."

"It's your risk, then, Miss Starbuck," the captain said. "And all I can do is wish you luck."

Klaus came across the deck at a run, carrying Jessie's rifle. He said nothing as he handed it to her. Jessie did not waste time examining the Winchester; she knew that its magazine held a full load. Stepping away from the two men, she levered a shell into the chamber and raised the rifle to her shoulder.

★

Chapter 10

Jessie swung the Winchester's muzzle toward her target as the steady rhythm of the ship's engine faded. The vessel started to lose weigh almost at once, and she realized that the captain had ordered the engine room to stop the vessel in order to give her a more stable footing when she fired. She spread her feet on the deck and pushed against the rail to double the advantage of the vessel's lessened rocking.

Raising her rifle, Jessie swung its muzzle along the high humped curve of the whale-shark's back. She lined the sights to the spot where she was sure a rifle slug would be most effective: the point where the front of the creature's huge gleaming form met the water's surface. The sharp downward curvature of its monstrously large back gave her the clue she needed to be sure that her bullets would drive into its head.

Satisfied at last, Jessie froze her stance. She held the

rifle's sights steadied on the spot she'd chosen as her target. She realized quite well that the odds of a killing shot were very heavily against her, and to equalize them as much as possible she held her firing stance for nearly a full minute while gauging the exact position of the spot she must hit on the bulking back of the whale-shark. Then in quick succession she let off the entire magazine load of high-velocity cartridges.

During the few moments that her volley lasted, Jessie pumped the Winchester's loading lever with smooth precision. Quickly but deliberately she shifted her point of aim after each shot in an effort to put as many of the slugs as possible into the monster's tiny fist-sized brain.

For several minutes the whale-shark did not move. Then as the bullets that had torn into its head continued to destroy its brain tissue, the creature's primitive nervous system responded. Humping its back, the whale-shark started threshing the water with its wide, spreading tail.

As soon as the Winchester's magazine was emptied, Jessie handed the gun to Klaus and reached for the second rifle. The whale-shark had not slackened its frantic gyrations, and now the placing of her follow-up shots required shifts in aiming and a faster finger on the weapon's trigger.

Time after time Jessie held her fire while she switched her point of aim, trying to make sure of letting off a telling shot. For many minutes after the magazine of the second rifle had been emptied, the big whale-shark continued to raise high rippling waves with its frantic dying spasms; then bit by bit its life slipped away until at last the movements of its huge form became less spastic and grew shorter in duration.

118

Jessie had lowered her rifle when the hammer clicked on the borrowed weapon's emptied magazine. She stood watching the great fish for a few moments until she was sure that its life was ebbing, then she turned to Captain Baker.

"I don't think we'll have to worry any longer," she told him. "It'll probably be several minutes before it stops splashing around, but I'm sure it won't be able to do any harm now."

"I'd say you're right," he agreed.

"Then let's get Ki and the boy out of that icy water before it chills them so badly that they'll be too cold to keep on swimming," she said.

"I haven't forgotten them," the captain assured her. "But there's one thing that I need to be sure of before we do anything else."

Baker turned and started across the deck toward the vessel's stern. After exchanging puzzled frowns, Jessie and Klaus followed. The captain reached the rear of the deck and glanced down briefly at the paddle wheel. He saw that it was rotating very slowly, just fast enough to hold the vessel in place against the current. Then he turned back to Jessie.

"Half the tricky job of rescuing someone who's gone overboard is to be sure the hands will get them back to the vessel without wasting any time," he explained. "And the best way to do that is to hold the ship steady in position so the men in the small boat can get back smoothly and quickly. Now, let's go take a look and see how that boat crew's doing."

Stopping at the rail, Baker began scanning the water for the small rowboat that had already put a substantial distance between itself and the ship. After a moment he turned back to Jessie, who had been searching the water with anxious eyes.

"I think the crew in the small boat have spotted your friends now," he told her. "It's stopped luffing around and is on a straight course."

While he was speaking, the captain raised his arm to point, and Jessie followed his hand's movement with her eyes. For a few seconds she saw nothing except the rippling creases of the sea's waves, then suddenly she spotted two small dots breaking the surface. They were close together, and she loosed a small sigh of relief.

"Ki's a strong swimmer," she said to Baker without taking her eyes off the dark little globes of the two heads that looked so far away. "I hope he can stay—" She broke off as the bow of the rowboat entered her field of vision, then went on, "I think they'll be all right. Your boat's quite close to them now."

"I can see that for myself," he agreed. He, too, kept his eyes on the boat approaching the two bobbing dots on the river's surface. "And the boat crew will have them out of the water in a jiffy. This isn't the first time my men have had to rescue some passenger who got careless."

"I will go to the below deck," Klaus volunteered. "I would wish to be there when the small boat arrives."

"Here on the upper deck we'll be able to see them better," Jessie said. "But I'll certainly come and join you below when they get closer."

As Klaus started toward the companionway, Captain Baker turned to Jessie and said, "If you don't mind waiting a minute or so to join your friend, I'd like to ask you how all this came about. I still don't know how that young boy fell overboard."

120

"He came here to the upper deck a minute or two ahead of his mother and fell on the deck when the ship rolled as it started to turn," Jessie explained.

"You were already here, then?"

"Yes, of course," she nodded. "Ki and Klaus and I had gotten here a few minutes earlier, and none of us was close enough to the boy to grab him when he fell down. The ship was tilting a bit at that moment, and the youngster just fell down and started rolling. He didn't—well, I suppose he wasn't able to stop himself until he fell off into the water. Then Ki jumped in to help him. I think you were in the wheelhouse at the time."

Before the captain could reply, the child's mother left the position at the corner of the wheelhouse where she had sought solitude. She came hurrying up to Jessie and the captain.

"Are you sure my boy's going to be saved?" she asked.

"Very sure," Jessie assured the woman before the captain could turn to face her. "Ki isn't going to let anything happen to him, and you can see for yourself that they're both all right, even if they are still in the water."

"Ki?" the woman frowned. "I don't understand."

"Ki is one of my party," Jessie explained. "His name is Japanese. Until my father died, Ki was his right-hand man, now he's continuing the same job for me."

Before Jessie could continue her explanation, Captain Baker turned to face the two women. "My men will take care—" he began. Then as he got a full look at the new arrival he broke off and exclaimed, "Mrs. Dalton! I didn't realize that you were aboard. Why didn't you let me know?"

"I was sure we'd run into one another sooner or later," she replied. "I certainly didn't realize that it would be under such nerve-wracking circumstances."

During the exchange between the two, Jessie had returned her attention to the river. When she saw that the boat had stopped and that Ki and the boy were being helped into it by the crew, she turned back to the captain and the new arrival.

"You can rest easily now," she told the mother. "Ki and your son are out of the water and safely in the boat."

"Oh, I'm so relieved!" Mrs. Dalton sighed. "James falling into the river was my fault; I simply wasn't paying enough attention to him."

"My apologies, Miss Starbuck," Baker said quickly. "I was so surprised to see Mrs. Dalton aboard that I've neglected to introduce you. Miss Starbuck, may I present Mrs. Jack Dalton, the wife of Nome's leading citizen. And I'm sure from what you've just heard us say that it's her youngster your friend Ki has saved from—"

Mrs. Dalton broke in quickly to say, "Now, let's not talk about ugly things that might've happened. My boy is safe, thanks to the quick action of you and your friend, Miss Starbuck. I don't know how to begin—"

"Please don't try to thank us," Jessie said. "It was just luck that we happened to be here at the right time."

Undeterred, Mrs. Dalton went on, "Of course, I'd have been happy to meet you under any circumstances, but knowing how greatly indebted I am to your companion, the one you call Ki, I'd like him to get back on board so I can thank him. It was a very dangerous thing he did, diving from this upper deck, and very courageous as well."

"No one's ever charged Ki with lack of courage," Jessie said. "I'm sure our feelings are pretty much the same. He's helped me out of unpleasant situations more times than I care to think about. I'm just glad that he was here to help you."

"But not half as glad as I am," Mrs. Dalton went on, frowning thoughtfully. She was an entirely different woman now than she'd been a moment earlier. Her voice showed no stress; her face no longer bore the worried frown. "Now, this man Ki who's been so brave and helpful, you said that he's an Oriental?"

"Yes." Jessie nodded. She did not repeat the details of Ki's relationship with her late father and now with herself.

"Then he'll be able to find quite a bit of company in Nome," Mrs. Dalton went on. "I'm sure that my husband is acquainted with most of the Orientals there."

Captain Baker had been dividing his attention between the position of the rescue boat and the pair in the water. Now he turned to volunteer, "Mrs. Dalton's husband, Jack, is the leading lawman of Nome. And a good man to have on your side in case you run into any trouble with the people there."

"My companions and I aren't going to Nome looking for trouble," Jessie told him. Then she added quickly, "And we certainly don't anticipate any. We're not going to be there very long. We'll be leaving for the back country as soon as we can get outfitted."

"If there's any way that Jack or I can help you while you're there, be sure to let us know," Mrs. Dalton offered.

"That's very kind of you," Jessic said. "But even if this is our first visit to Alaska, we're not strangers to the outdoors. I have a ranch in Texas, and the country down there can be as—well, not as wild as Alaska, but not far behind. We won't be in Nome very long. We're going on into the interior as soon as we've bought the supplies and the extra gear we'll need."

Shouts began rising from the lower deck before their conversation could be continued, and Baker said, "That rescue boat must be getting pretty close by this time. I'd better get to the lower deck. Now, I'm sure that's where you ladies feel you ought to be, too, but I'm going to ask you to stay up on this deck until he's safely aboard."

A frown burst full-blown on Martha Dalton's face, and Jessie saw that she was about to protest. She said quickly, "I'll stay with Mrs. Dalton and keep her company while the small boat's getting back here to the ship."

Mrs. Dalton choked back whatever protest she'd started to make, but when she did speak her voice showed the strain she was under as she said, "I want to see my boy the minute that boat gets near enough."

"Let me just stay here with you. It'll be quite a while before the small boat gets back, and the passengers will very likely find out that it's your boy out there. Then they'll keep you so busy talking that you won't be able to watch."

"Miss Starbuck's offer makes sense," Baker said quickly. "And I'll be on the lower deck when he comes aboard. I'll bring him to you just as quickly as I can."

"I suppose you're right," Martha Dalton agreed.

"Good." He nodded. "Now, just be as patient as possible, and I'll have your boy up here as soon as he's safely on board."

As the captain started away, Mrs. Dalton turned back to Jessie and said, "I'm sure we'll be talking again before we get to Nome, but just in case we don't, I hope you'll remember my invitation."

"I certainly intend to," Jessie agreed.

"Of course," Mrs. Dalton said. She was silent for a moment, then went on, "You appear to be the sort of independent woman that I am, Miss Starbuck. If I'm not mistaken, you've learned that the only way to handle men when they're trying to tell you what to do is to listen to them and do what you please."

"I might not go that far," Jessie said. "But if you're suggesting that I make up my mind and follow my own decisions, you're right."

"Good. Then would you like to come with me?"

"Where?" Jessie frowned.

"To the lower deck, where they're getting ready to bring my son on board. I intend to be there when he steps on the ship."

Jessie saw that she had no alternative. She nodded her agreement and kept abreast of the anxious mother as she hurried down the few steps to the boat's main deck. As their descent of the steps brought the narrow strip of the lower deck into view, Jessie gasped when she saw that except for a space at the gangway, which was being kept clear by men of the vessel's crew, the narrow strip of deck between the rail and the cabin doors was packed with passengers.

She realized at once what had happened. News of the child's fall into the water and the impending arrival of his rescue crew had spread among the passengers. Now, they were flocking to the spot to get first look at the returning boat. On the step below her, Martha Dalton had stopped, too.

Martha was not at all deterred. She began pushing and elbowing her way through the jammed-together cluster of milling passengers, with Jessie following in her wake. They reached a point where the onlookers were sardined so tightly that even the pushing and sidling moves attempted by Jessie and Martha Dalton could not take them any farther. After they'd elbowed and tugged and shoved for several minutes without success, Martha turned to Jessie.

"I don't like to do this," she said determinedly, "but we're not going to be able to pass through unless I use some drastic measures."

"I'm afraid I don't understand what you mean by drastic measures," Jessie frowned.

"You will, very quickly. Just stay close behind me, Jessie."

Jessie nodded, even though she still could get no idea of what her companion was planning to do. However, Martha Dalton's intention became clear almost at once. She managed to wriggle and squeeze her arms upwards, until she could reach her narrow-brimmed felt hat, and removed the eight-inch-long pin that secured it to her head. Then with a skill that would have done credit to an expert duelist, she brought the hatpin down and quickly jabbed it in turn into the buttocks of the two men just ahead of her and Jessie.

Reacting to the piercing bite of the needle-sharp pin, the men who'd been stabbed began shoving away those closest to them. Their greater strength and bulk accomplished what the efforts of the two women had been unable to bring about, and created a small area of open space in spite of the crowd.

In the miniature melee that followed, as Martha Dalton plied her pin for the second and third time, Jessie and her mentor were able to squeeze through the gaps opened by the spectators' sudden movements until they reached the space that the ship's crewmen had been keeping free for the rowboat to berth.

Jessie saw Klaus after a moment, standing at the front of the packed group of onlookers, away from the cleared area where the crewmen were waiting. At his feet was a pile of cordage, and a second quick glance revealed it to be a rope ladder.

Now Jessie remembered that Klaus had been one of the first to reach the spot, that he'd accompanied the crew members dispatched to handle the rowboat's landing. Because he was recognized as belonging to her party, he had been allowed by Captain Baker to remain with the crew members waiting for the small boat to reach the *Sequoia*.

Then Klaus saw Jessie and Martha Dalton and hurried to join them. As he drew close enough to be heard above the babble of voices from the onlookers, he said, "I looked for you, but when I did not see you, I thought perhaps you would to the top deck have gone."

"I don't suppose there'd have been any more room on the upper deck than there is here," she replied.

"You are here just in time," he went on, turning and gesturing toward the water. "There, you can see Ki's face almost."

Jessie and Martha turned to follow Klaus's gesture. The rowboat was indeed close, the men at the oars sending it in a fast pace in spite of being forced to buck the current. Ki was in the prow, his arms cradling the huddled-up figure of the blanket-wrapped boy he'd saved. He was not looking toward the boat; his attention was focused on the little knot of deckhands who were beginning to lower the rope ladder into the water.

Then the vessel's deck line cut off her view as the prow of the small boat thumped into the side of the ship. Almost at once the air was filled with the garbled noise of shouts, which were now being exchanged between the rescue party and the deckhands who were helping its members aboard.

"I'm going to the rail to get my child back," Martha Dalton said. "There'll be lots of time for us to talk again before the ship gets to Nome. I'm not even going to do more than say 'thank you' now, but—"

"Seeing your child safe is all the thanks we need," Jessie broke in to tell her. "As you said, we'll have plenty of time to talk later on."

"I'm very glad this little accident has had such a happy ending," Jessie told Klaus as she watched the rescued child being helped up on the ship's deck by one of the men who'd knelt to reach down to the youngster.

"It would not have ended so well if Ki had not leaped into the sea at once, or if your good shooting had not made sure that the big shark would not be able to attack them," Klaus pointed out.

"That was just a matter of us being in the right place at the right time," Jessie said. "And anybody would've done—"

She broke off as Ki's head and shoulders appeared above the edge of the deck, and Martha Dalton reached the head of the ladder just in time to bend down and grasp the rescued youngster, to lift him from Ki's arms. An explosion of shouts arising from the crowd of passengers made it impossible for Jessie and Klaus to carry on a conversation. They watched in silence while a pair of deckhands began clearing the way for Martha to carry the little boy to their cabin. Then the spectators began to turn away, scattering or forming little knots to rehash the incident.

Bucking the tide of the departing passengers, Jessie and Klaus made their way to the head of the ladder. Ki was standing there, wearing only his breachclout. He looked at them, a smile breaking out on his usually taciturn face.

"I would not advise that either of you bathe in this water," he said. "I am going to my cabin, to put on dry clothing, but also to escape the attention of the passengers. I will join you later, at dinner, after I have gotten warm again."

★

Chapter 11

"And that's Nome?" Jessie asked Martha Dalton when the boat's intermittent whistling ended.

"You're not seeing all of the town, Jessie," Martha Dalton replied. "What you're looking at now is just a small part of Nome. Don't judge the town by its waterfront; that's its worst feature. Wait until you get to shore and can see the sections back from the bay."

Jessie nodded absently without looking away from the shoreline. She and Martha were standing at the ship's rail, gazing at the higgledy-piggledy gaggle of buildings that occupied the narrow strip of land along the waterfront. With two or three exceptions, the buildings that she could see were shoddy and dilapidated. Even the larger ones seemed to have been thrown together using any bits and pieces of lumber that the builder had been able to scrounge from a junk pile.

If there was one of them that had been constructed from new lumber by skilled carpenters, it was not visible from the vessel, and the weathered wood of the walls on all the buildings hinted that paint in Nome was an unknown commodity. Along the land's edge, short piers protruded the least possible distance into the water which would allow a ship to come alongside them.

"Since it's such a new town, I somehow got the idea that Nome would look new and raw, with a lot of houses made from freshly cut lumber," she told her companion.

"None of the men have been interested in logging since the gold craze hit this part of Alaska," Martha said.

"I can understand that," Jessie replied. "Gold fever's really an insidious disease."

She was still watching the new vistas that opened as the ship moved past the throat of the bay and headed toward the line of a half-dozen short piers, spaced as closely together as possible at the edge of the water. Only two of the piers were unoccupied, ships bearing the designations of a dozen ports from every point of the compass occupied the others.

Behind the buildings, dwarfing them by the grandeur of its bulk, a row of cliffs rose. From the angle at which the ship was approaching, their gray rock sides had appeared at first to thrust toward the sky in an unbroken vertical rise. Now Jessie could see that in small niches that occurred here and there a few tatterdemalion houses had been erected. They did not seem to follow any kind of road or path but nestled wherever a ledge protruding from the escarpment offered space for them.

Before Jessie could take in the entire panorama that spread before her, the vessel altered its course and began to head for one of the empty berths on the shore. Now she could see that what had seemed a few minutes earlier to be a single imposing granite promontory was actually a series of cliffs broken by deep, narrow gulches. In the slitted cuts between them she could see the roofs of houses against the streaked white remnants of last winter's still unmelted snow.

"I was prepared for it to be cold up here, but I didn't realize that the country was so terribly rough," Jessie told her companion. "As I've told you, my only acquaintance with Alaska until now has been much further south, where it's more a part of the continent."

Martha nodded. "That's where my husband made his reputation as a lawman, in Juneau. He pinned on his first badge there, and I don't suppose we'd ever have left if it hadn't been for some cheap politicians who came to dislike him because he wouldn't give their cronies special favors."

"Ever since we first met, I've intended to ask you if your husband has any relatives left in the States," Jessie said. "I know there's a . . . " she hesitated, then stopped and a frown formed on her face.

Before Jessie could find more kindly words than those which had first come into her mind, Martha said, "You're not the first person to wonder if Jack has any family ties to the outlaws in the Dalton gang that's so notorious in the west. I've heard about them, of course, but all I can tell you is that if Jack's related to them, he's hidden it even from me."

"You've never asked him, then?"

"No. I've hinted, but I haven't found the courage to ask any direct questions. If Jack's caught on to my hints, he hasn't shown it. You see, Jessie, we're not yet what you'd call a closely knit family. Jack and I first got acquainted right before we moved to Nome from Juneau. He was . . . well, I suppose you'd say he was driven out by a bunch of unfriendly politicians who were afraid he'd expose their ties to the criminals that really ran the town. We've been married less than a year."

"But, your son . . . !" Jessie's exclamation popped out before she'd had time to consider it.

"I was a widow when I married Jack," Martha explained. "When my first husband died, I felt I'd need a man to help me raise my boy, so when Jack started courting me . . . well, I just didn't observe the conventional mourning period and said I'd marry him. Then Jack's troubles in Juneau started, soon after our wedding, and . . . well, I'm hoping that up here where he hasn't any political enemies, we'll really become a family."

"I'm sorry," Jessie told her. "I didn't mean to pry."

"And I shouldn't be loading you down with my problems. Perhaps we'd better talk about something else, Jessie, if you don't mind."

"Of course I don't. Suppose you tell me a little bit about Nome. We won't be staying here long, a day or two at most, but I'm sure you'll know the best place for us to buy the supplies we'll be needing."

"I haven't had a chance to learn much about Nome in the short time Jack and I have been here," Martha said. "Jack will be able to help you more than I can. There are so many rough characters up here that he doesn't like for me to go into town—such as it is—unless he goes with me."

"Anything that will save us time will be a big help. The less time we spend here, the sooner we'll be able to head back to Texas, where my ranch needs my attention," Jessie told her. "I'd be happy if we could start for the interior tomorrow."

"Up here, they call it the outback. I try to remember to do the same thing, but I'm not really a native yet."

"Well, I can understand that." Jessie smiled. "But it certainly isn't what I'd expected to find. I suppose there's a hotel or rooming house where the three of us can get a room for a day or two, while we're getting the supplies we'll need?"

"I'm afraid you're asking the impossible, Jessie. Here in Nome right now men are sleeping five and six to a room in all the boarding houses and hotels, on the floor and in the halls. All of them are waiting for ships that are bringing the supplies and gear they need to start for the outback."

"I should have thought about that sooner," Jessie said. "But I didn't have any idea what to expect here in Nome."

"I think the best thing we can do is to stop by Jack's office and ask him what you should do. He knows the town much better than I do, and he just might be able to find a place where you and your friends can stay."

Jessie looked around the cramped little cubicle that served as Jack Dalton's office and thought about sardines packed in their cans. Near the desk that left only inches of floor space between it and the wall, Martha and her husband were locked in an embrace. Jessie, Ki and Klaus were lined up along the raw unpainted boards on the opposite side of the tiny cramped room.

At last the Daltons broke away from their prolonged hug and the kisses that went with it. Martha made the appropriate introductions and followed them quickly by giving her husband a short summary of the narrow escape her son had

135

on the voyage and the roles that Jessie and Ki had played in his rescue.

"I sent the boy on home ahead of me," she concluded, "because Miss Starbuck and her companions need somewhere to sleep tonight, and I thought perhaps you could—"

"Find them a room for the night," Dalton broke in to finish for her.

Jack Dalton was not a tall man, but his build was sturdy. His square-jawed face was reddened by exposure to biting winds and driving snows. Even indoors he had not taken off his heavy knee-length fur-outside deerskin coat or the Colt .45 belted in a holster that dangled almost to midthigh.

"There's no hope at all that your friends can find a place to stay here in Nome, Miss Starbuck, and I'm sorry to say this after what Martha's told me," Dalton went on, turning to Jessie as he spoke. "The snow-melt—such as it is—has just started. Men heading for the outback are sleeping in the halls in the few rooming houses that there are here in Nome, and in chairs in the saloons, which we've got plenty of. Those who aren't lucky enough to find a roof to sleep under are spreading their bedrolls in the alleys and on what little level land there is outside town."

"I suppose I should have realized how crowded it would be here in Nome," Jessie said a bit ruefully. "But we won't suffer too much. As soon as we get our luggage off the ship—" She stopped and shook her head, then went on, "I've been so interested in looking at Nome that I hadn't thought about much of anything else until now. The ship will have to unload whatever cargo it's carrying, and that can't be done in what's left of the day. We can stay aboard tonight."

"Even if you could find a decent place to stay, you'll

likely sleep better on the ship than you would on shore, Miss Starbuck." Dalton nodded. "Things get pretty rough here in town when a ship's just docked, especially a passenger ship."

"I suppose most of the stores open early?" Jessie asked. "We'll need to buy the supplies we'll need before we can start for what you people up here call the outback."

"Night's the same as day up in this part of Alaska," Dalton replied. "This evening, sunset won't begin until nearly midnight, and always when a ship's just come in things are a little wilder than usual in the saloons and gambling houses and—" He stopped short, then went on, " . . . and the red light district. I won't even get a chance to go to bed tonight."

"Then Ki and Klaus and I will just go back to the ship and get a good night's rest," Jessie said. "And early tomorrow morning we'll get an early start for the outback."

Klaus and Jessie had both been so exhausted from their ecstatically prolonged embraces that they couldn't think of anything except rest, so they'd tried to go to sleep. They found—as they had on other similar occasions during the voyage—that sleep was impossible when they tried to stretch out side by side in the cramped, narrow bunk.

Klaus had departed reluctantly to go to his own cabin, and after turning the small lever that locked her door from inside the stateroom, Jessie had returned to her bunk. Pleasantly exhausted from the hours she and Klaus had so recently shared, she was dropping off to sleep when the metallic clicking of the lock broke the night's silence.

Thinking that after Klaus left he'd gotten an infusion of fresh vigor and decided to return, Jessie did not stir. Instead, she feigned sleep, for she'd come to relish Klaus's unconventional methods of awakening her with subtle caresses of his lips and tongue.

She kept her eyes closed for several moments, waiting for her lover. Then she opened them to a slit, watching for Klaus to enter and anticipating her pleasure when he'd begin to arouse her with his agile tongue and moist, warm lips. The door opened noiselessly and Jessie's eyes flew wide when she realized that the black shadow outlined by the starlight in the cabin's narrow doorway was not Klaus's silhouette, but that of a bulking stranger.

Her holstered Colt was swinging from the clothes hook on the wall beside her bunk. Jessie reached for it, and as the intruder stepped inside the cabin, she said levelly, "Get out of my cabin this minute, or I'll shoot you."

"Now, a nice lady like you wouldn't do that," the intruder replied. His cajoling, whispered words were belied by his hoarsely rasping voice.

"I've warned you once," Jessie told him. "I've got a gun in my hand, and I won't waste my breath a second time."

"You ain't the only one that's got a gun," the man snarled.

Jessie saw the plug-ugly's arm coming up in a move to draw even before he'd stopped speaking. She triggered off a shot as his hand was closing on the butt of his revolver. The intruder's frame jerked backward as her slug went home. His gunhand sagged, and the revolver he'd managed to free from its holster, in the moment before Jessie's shot tore into him, dropped to the deck with a clatter. Then he crumpled and fell in an ungainly sprawl.

Reverberations from Jessie's shot filled the tiny cabin and were still ringing in her ears when the whispery patter of bare feet sounded on the deck outside and Ki's voice came through the darkness of the deck.

"Jessie! Are you all right?"

"As right as possible," she replied as Ki's familiar silhouette filled the cabin's narrow doorway.

Other noises were breaking the night by this time. Above the patter of Ki's bare feet on the deck outside she could hear more distant sounds from the other cabins close by.

Ki stepped over the intruder's motionless form to strike a match and light the oil lamp in its binnacle on the wall beside the bed. A quick glance showed him that Jessie was getting to her feet, reaching for the crumpled bed sheet. He took the half step necessary to reach her and helped her to drape the sheet over her shoulders.

"I'm quite all right, Ki," Jessie said calmly.

"What happened?" he asked.

Before Jessie could reply, Klaus came running up. He saw the dead man sprawled out on deck and looked up to face her as he asked, "You are not hurt?"

"I'm quite all right," Jessie assured him. She gestured toward the intruder and said calmly, "You can see for yourself. He must've had a passkey or a picklock of some kind. I was half asleep when—" She broke off as the patter of feet sounded on the deck, overriding the more distant sounds of voices from other cabins. Then she went on, "We'll have a crowd here in a minute, Ki. Please close the door and stand in front of it until I can slip on my robe."

Before Ki had the door completely closed, Captain Baker's voice reached Jessie. She stepped behind the shielding door and looked around its edge as the captain stopped in front of it. He glanced from the dead intruder's body to Jessie.

"Are you all right, Miss Starbuck?" he asked.

"Quite all right, Captain," she replied calmly. "That man got my stateroom door open; I suppose he used a picklock or had a passkey. I keep my pistol handy when I'm in strange places, and when he threatened me with his gun I shot him."

"And quite rightly, too," Baker said. "I've sent one of the deck watch to find the sheriff. I'm sure you won't have anything to worry about. Stay in your cabin, if you want to avoid a lot of questions before he gets here."

By the time Jessie had donned a robe and slid her feet into the bedroom slippers that were on the floor beside the bunk, Ki's voice was drowned out by the babble of excited questions from the passengers who still remained on board the *Sequoia*. Then the louder, more authoritative voice of Captain Baker rose above the lesser sound, and bit by bit the other voices faded. Jessie waited until the flurry of voices faded to a whispering undertone, then she opened the door.

"Are you sure you're all right, Miss Starbuck?" Baker asked.

"Of course I'm all right, Captain," Jessie replied. Behind him she could see that a short distance away on both sides of her cabin door the deck was still crowded with curious passengers. She went on, "I'm sorry to have caused so much excitement, but I wasn't going to allow that man I shot to get in here and maul me around."

"Of course not," Baker agreed. "That would've been unthinkable. I'll have the deckhands on night watch drag the fellow's body away until the local authorities can send to—"

"You don't have to worry about that, Captain." A man's voice rose above the babble of of the passengers. "I'll take care of everything that's necessary."

Jessie recognized the voice as that of the Sheriff Dalton, and by the time she'd slipped on her robe and stepped outside to the deck, Dalton had succeeded in pushing his way through the crowd. Though most of the passengers had left, there was still a small group clustered at a distance on both sides of the door where Jessie and Baker and Ki were standing. Dalton turned back to face the onlookers.

"All the excitement's over," he announced. "You folks get back to your cabins, because there's not going to be anything more for you to look at." He waited until they began moving away before turning again to face the three at the door and asking, "I guess it was one of you that shot the fellow over there?"

"I did," Jessie replied. "He'd opened my cabin door with a passkey and was starting to come inside. He didn't realize that I had my Colt handy."

"Nobody's going to blame you, Miss Starbuck," Dalton assured Jessie. "And I hope you don't figure that I wasn't tending to my job the way I ought to."

Captain Baker broke in to say, "If you don't need me here any longer, Sheriff, I'll get a couple of men to drag that body over by the gangway. I suppose there'll be somebody coming to take it off the ship?"

"Just as soon as I can get back on shore and send the undertaker after it," Dalton assured him. As the captain turned to leave, Dalton picked up his interrupted conversation with Jessie. "The fact is," he went on, "there's just too many of these drifters here in Nome for me to keep them corralled up the way they ought to be, right now especially, when they're waiting for the ice to melt in the high country outback where they're heading to prospect."

"Of course, that's where we're heading, too," Jessie said.

"But Ki and Klaus and I can handle just about anything we're likely to run into."

"After seeing what you did a little while ago, I can't keep from agreeing with you." Dalton nodded. "But I'm keeping you and your friends standing here losing sleep that you're going to need when you start out. Now, I'm going to ask a favor of you, if you don't mind."

"Not in the least," Jessie told him. "What is it you want?"

"You'll be coming back here when you finish up whatever's taking you to the outback?"

"Why, certainly," she replied. "It's the only port I know of in this part of the territory, and we've got to get back home as soon as our job here is finished."

"Then if you don't mind, be sure to stop by my office," Dalton went on. "I've got an idea that I'd appreciate you listening to."

"Of course I will," Jessie nodded. "We'll probably have to wait for a boat to take us back to the States."

"Then I'll be looking to see you," Dalton told her. "Now, if you and your friends will excuse me, I've got to tend to my job."

As Dalton started toward the gangway, Klaus turned to Jessie, a puzzled frown on his face as he asked, "Please to tell me, Jessie, of what do you suppose a man like Jack Dalton would want with you to talk?"

"I haven't any more of an idea than you do, Klaus," she answered. "But I'd be willing to bet it'll be interesting. Now, let's try to get some sleep. We've got some very busy days ahead of us."

★

Chapter 12

"I'll tell you one thing, Ki," Jessie said. "Before we started getting ready for this trip to the outback, I never dreamed the day would come when I'd pay a thousand dollars for a scrubby little run-of-the-mill jenny."

"Yes, the price surprised me, too," Ki agreed.

"But this is the time we needed one." She went on, "And now that we've found it's so well broken in, I'm glad we bought it."

They were standing beside the diminutive donkey, where they'd halted for a breathing spell at the wide and sparsely forested crest of a rise in the broken landscape. Beyond, they could see that the depressions in the humps that broke the flatness of the plain, which they would be crossing to the next sawtooth ledge, still contained streaks and patches of snow that even now at the peak of summer had not melted.

For the past hour or more the three had been laboriously climbing a steep upslope, and the sight of the relatively flat prairie had been very welcome. Jessie was standing beside Ki while he looped to a pine sapling the reins of the undersized pack mule she'd bought before leaving Nome, after trying in vain to find a horse that was for sale.

When Ki only smiled at her remark, Jessie went on, "I was surprised to find out that there are so few horses in Alaska, but after learning what the climate here does to them I can understand the reason. Right this minute I'd gladly pay twice as much for a good horse—or three good horses—as I did for this little jenny."

"So would I, and very gladly," Ki agreed.

"Tell me please, why it is you call this *maultier* a jenny," Klaus asked, a puzzled frown on his face. He was following the example of Jessie and Ki, easing off the straps of his bulky backpack and letting it slip to the ground. "It is not a word which in my own language I can recall."

"You speak French, Klaus" Jessie smiled. "I'm sure you'll recognize the word *gennet*."

"Yes, of course, it is a young female horse," Klaus replied. Then the frown rippled off his face as he went on, "Aha, now I can understand. Even someone with a knowledge of your language no greater than mine can see very easily how the word becomes changed."

While they were talking the pack mule they'd been discussing had started nuzzling away the snow around a pine tree's roots, seeking the tender grass shoots that were beginning to sprout under the white crust that still covered much of the ground.

Jessie turned and tilted her head to gaze at the long incline that rose ahead of them. She said, "We've spent the better part of an hour getting to the end of that last upslope, and I suppose this one will be about the same. I'm not quite sure it's noon, with the sun acting the way it does up here at this time of the year, but wouldn't it be a good time to eat, now that we've stopped?"

"In this always daylight, I find myself being always hungry," Klaus told her. "A bite of sausage and a crust of bread I would very much enjoy."

"I'll vote with you, Klaus," Ki agreed. "If we take the time to eat something now, we might be able to push on a little further than we'd anticipated before stopping again. I don't mind admitting I'm anxious to get to the little lake that shows on Alex's map, because until we do we can't begin checking the survey's notes."

Ki was moving toward the pack mule as he spoke. He brought out the food parcel they were using and placed it on the ground near them. Unwinding the oilskin in which their victuals were wrapped, Ki gestured an invitation for Jessie and Klaus to help themselves; then he picked the food he wanted for his own meal and settled down beside them. For the next few minutes they were silent, munching cheese and sausage and crackers while they surveyed the rugged terrain that they would be forced to cross before they reached their destination.

While they ate they studied the distant vista and surveyed the serrated hill crests that still rose ahead of them. There was little difference between those ahead and those they'd struggled over in order to reach their present stopping place. No sign of settlement was visible on the broken terrain, and there were no paths or trails branching off the one they'd been following.

With nothing new to catch their attention they soon turned

to watching the steady perseverance shown by their own jenny in seeking food. It was now swinging its head in small arcs, grazing diligently on the grass shoots that its snow clearing had uncovered.

"To our bad fortune it is that we cannot eat as readily as the animals do," Klaus said after a moment or two. "Think of the ease we would have in climbing without our packs if directly from the earth itself we could get our food."

"I suppose you're right." Jessie smiled. "But I'll still take bread and bacon instead of grass. I'm just glad that we've been able to move as fast as we have, carrying these heavy packs."

With Nome well behind them after three days of steady uphill hiking, the high land which now stretched ahead of them did not seem to be as challenging as it had when they first set out. Beyond the ridge where they had stopped, the towering crests of still higher ridges were visible. These rose above the slopes broken by the humped foothills of a mountain range. Its peaks were completely snow-blanketed and were much higher than those which lay closer to their present position. The nearest ridges were challenging enough, for their faces showed little signs of snow, an indication that they must be almost vertical cliffs of solid rock.

Between the high mountains and the spot where they'd chosen to stop, Jessie, Ki and Klaus saw a vista of recurring ridges, most of them still half-covered with snow even in the middle of the brief Alaskan summer. Few of the closer formations were higher than the one on whose crest they'd stopped to rest, but the continued upslope of the terrain was more than a hint that their travel would not be any easier ahead than it had been while crossing the broken country they had already encountered.

There was little vegetation to obscure their view. At the altitude they'd now reached the trees no longer covered the ground but grew in small patches rather than in large, unbroken, densely forested spreads. After having pushed through several areas where the forest was thick, they'd learned to avoid such places. Between the trees on these constantly shaded expanses the snow was usually still piled up in deep unmelted drifts, and in such places their progress was always slowed to a muscle-challenging crawl.

"Unless I've been misreading Alex's map, it can't be too much farther to his claim marker," Jessie remarked as they were finishing their impromptu meal. "Another two days, three at the most, I'd say, should see us to the end of our trip."

"Do you think the food we have brought will last until we get back to Nome?" Klaus asked.

"It'll have to," she replied. "Even if we have to ration ourselves pretty severely. But there are two things in our favor. On the way back we'll be going downhill and we'll also be following the same trail. Now that we know what it's like, we'll be able to move faster."

"Speaking of moving faster," Ki put in, "we'd better get started again."

Accustomed to the task after the days they'd already spent, they lost little time getting the pack mule reloaded. Then they resumed their slow progress on the winding trail, which hugged the base of the string of humped hillocks that curved toward the nearest of the mountain's ridges and took them steadily uphill.

As the sun swung around toward the low peaks that would hide its face when it reached them in its summer-shortened arc, they came upon one of the many small mountain lakes that dotted the miniature meadows that spread in patches of level land from the bases of the frequent rises.

Even in the relatively short distance they'd now covered, the trail they were following had steadily become more erratic. It was not as well defined as those in places that were easier to reach, and it had also become fainter over the years. More than once they'd encountered areas where it had disappeared almost completely.

In such places they'd been forced to abandon their earlier custom of traveling in a compact group. They'd learned early in their trip that instead of keeping on the zigzagging trail, they would find easier going if they spread the distance between each other. Moving with wide spaces between them enabled the one closest to a sharply winding curved section of foot-and-hoof-packed earth could signal the others to follow.

Klaus was nearest of the three to the little mountain lake they encountered an hour or more after they'd made their lunch stop. The small pond of water was no novelty; they'd already passed several in the small mountain meadows. At his first glimpse of the water's shining surface he'd signaled to Jessie and Ki by stopping and waving his arms.

When Klaus was sure that he had their attention, he pointed to the lake and gestured for them to join him, then hunkered down at the water's edge and scooped up a few palms full of water to drink. After their first few days on the trail, they'd learned that the cool, thin, dry air of the Alaskan high country was as dehydrating as the hot air to which they were accustomed on the hot Texas prairies.

"We've been on this flat section of the trail for quite a while," Ki said as he and Jessie and Klaus got within easy speaking distance. "We're certainly getting very close to the marking stakes that I'm sure Alex put out."

"Yes. We must be in the area where he did his prospecting," Jessie agreed. "My guess is that we've traveled just about the same distance that I remember him mentioning in the stories he told me about his Alaskan days."

"Then don't you think it might be a good idea for me to angle up and start looking closely at those little foothill humps?" Ki went on. "I can see a lot more land from the top of one of those rises, and I might just be lucky enough to spot one of the claim stakes he set out."

"Do you believe that after so many years have passed the stakes would yet be undisturbed?" Klaus frowned.

"I'd almost be willing to guarantee they would be," Ki nodded.

"Of course they would, Klaus," Jessie said. "When I was a very little girl, Alex used to tell me—well, I suppose you'd call them bedtime stories—about his days here in Alaska. And one of the things he mentioned every now and then was how dangerous it was for anyone to disturb the stakes that marked a claim. He said that more men were killed for doing that than for stealing another prospector's grub sack."

"But is it not murder to kill a man for such a small thing as moving a stake to a claim?" Klaus frowned.

"No, indeed," Jessie replied. "Claim jumping here in Alaska was a more serious crime than murder. It was exactly as it had been during the days of the forty-niners in the mainland west. If a prospector there caught a claim jumper moving his original stakes, he knew that he could shoot the man who was guilty without having to worry about standing trial for murder."

"Jessie's right," Ki agreed. "Why, being called a claim jumper was as big an insult as being called a horse thief or a cattle rustler was later on."

Klaus shook his head. "When I was a young boy reading stories of your American West in the books of Karl May, I have read about such things, but never did I believe they really could be true."

"They were true enough, I'm sure," Jessie said.

"Then if we have gotten so close, and there are the stakes still in place, we should of course begin to look for them." Klaus nodded. "This is why my father has insisted that we come here. I must his eyes be in confirming the claim for the coal deposit and investigating it so that we can agree with you on a price our firm will be willing to pay for it."

"We'd better split up again when we start out," Jessie said. She waved her arm in a sweeping gesture that took in the low ridge that ran along the crest at the end of the broad clearing, and went on, "Ki, suppose you go to the far edge, as you suggested earlier. Klaus, you take the rest of the right-hand side and half the center, and I'll go on from here."

Ki had already gotten to his feet. Now he gestured a good-bye to Jessie and Klaus before starting toward the ridge that broke the ground line at the rise of its base and the sky-line with its jagged crest. Between him and the land line of the ridge there were several thick growths of brush. Ki began moving in a deliberately patternless zigzagging when he reached them, choosing the direction where the terrain promised be the easiest for him to cross.

He stopped at each clump of the tall stands of brush to pull aside the branches and glance quickly at the ground that was hidden by them. He knew that Alex had followed the example of many early prospectors in putting an additional marker to his discovery stake—which was also his claim stake—in some spot where it would be unnoticed.

This was his insurance, a precaution that would enable him to prove his discovery rights if some desperate or crooked prospector who'd reached the spot later decided to break the law and replace an earlier prospector's claim with an outlaw stake of his own.

Stopping as often as he did, Ki consumed more time and covered less distance than he'd intended. After a half-hour or more had passed, he realized with a start that he was only half as close to the ridge as he'd planned to be. He speeded his pace and chose his path more carefully. Only one large clump of brush now stood between him and the ridge.

He had hurried to its edge, pulled the springy outer limbs of the big brush stand apart and was well into the undergrowth when a deep, rumbling growl sounded from the tangle of vegetation. The rumbles ended in a snarl as less than a dozen feet in front of him the head and shoulders of an immense bear rose, towering above the top of the brush in front of him. The hulking creature fitted the descriptions Alex Starbuck had given Ki of an Alaskan grizzly. Erect on its hind feet, the bear's broad, humped shoulders were almost two feet above Ki's head, and the fearsomely clawed paws, in which its heavily muscled forelegs ended, rose several inches above Ki's shoulders.

In the instant after Ki saw the grizzly, he turned to run, but as he swiveled around, the loose, baggy fabric of one of his trouser legs was snagged by the sharp end of a broken limb low in the tangle of brush. Ki kicked hard, trying to liberate himself, but the heavy branches would not break no matter how strongly he kicked and pulled; nor would the closely woven cloth tear free.

As yet the grizzly had not started toward him. It stood swaying from side to side, turning its broad, massive head, the nostrils of its glistening black snout opening wide and then closing to slits as it sniffed the still air, seeking Ki's scent. Now and then it opened its mouth wide in its gulping breathing. In the few quick glances Ki allowed himself as he bent forward, trying to free his trouser leg from the snagging brush, he could see the big creature's red tongue between two fearsome sets of long, yellowed fangs.

He realized quite well that his unarmed combat skills were useless to him against such a massive and heavily muscled antagonist. Even when he delivered his most crushing blows, he knew they would be no more than small annoyances to such a thick-coated, powerful creature.

Though the points of his *shuriken* were needle-sharp, and the edges of the star-shaped throwing blades razor-keen, they would be no more than annoying mosquito bites after going through the bear's heavy fur and thick skin. Only his *bo* remained, and its short blade was little longer than the bear's heavy claws.

Ki also realized that he had little time remaining, for the bear had now located the source of the human scent and was moving toward him. The whipping branches disturbed by its advance were slapping against its fur and skin, but this was no more than a minor annoyance. Its massive paws crushed the brush as it crashed through it. The hulking animal was not walking on all fours but moved erect, as a man would walk, its huge padded hind feet crushing the small lower twigs of the undergrowth as it advanced with low, shuffling steps.

Ki had not given up his efforts to tear free. His constant tugging finally frayed the closely woven cloth enough to release him. In the instant before the bear's outstretched forepaws could grasp him in their fatal embrace, Ki dropped to the ground and levered himself just out of reach of the grizzly's huge paws.

Rumbling growls burst from the beast's throat as its claws scraped even deeper tracks in the dirt while its huge jaws closed on empty air. Before it could lift itself to move closer, Ki loosed a *shuriken*. The twirling throwing blade went home. It sliced into the grizzly's glistening black nose and remained lodged there even after the animal opened its mouth wide to loose a rumbling roar of pain. Ki had his second blade ready an instant after he'd thrown the first. He saw his opportunity at once and quickly flicked the blade into the beast's yawning mouth.

Twirling in its short shining arc, the *shuriken* hit its target. Its razor-sharp teeth cut a slit in the bear's tongue, and then the animal closed its yawning jaws, trying to crush the slicing blade. Its own effort spelled the grizzly's doom as it tried vainly to close its huge jaws. The pressure of its own jaws closing drove the firmly lodged blade into the animal's upper palate. Its needled tips and the razor-sharp, saw-toothed edges sliced through the palate's layer of thin bone covered by soft gristle. The trickle of blood started by the *shuriken's* steel cutting tips became a flood.

Only a few seconds passed before spurts of blood began to gush from the grizzly's yawning jaws as the tip of the blade's points stabbed into back of the animal's tongue and severed the big veins on the bottom of its mouth. At the same time the uppermost arc of the *shuriken* was driven more deeply into the beast's huge head.

Now the grizzly forgot about Ki. It began clawing at its mouth in a vain effort to dislodge the *shuriken*, but its frantic clawing only drove the blade deeper. The blood was trickling freely from its mouth by this time, but an even greater flow was gushing down the animal's throat. Its growls became bubbling gargles as it clawed even more fiercely at its jaws, trying to stop the gushing flow of blood that was filling its throat, choking it and cutting off the air on which its life depended, drowning the big bear in its own blood.

Ki had another *shuriken* in his fingers and was waiting to send it sailing to the first vulnerable spot that the bear exposed in its struggles. The animal was ignoring him now, forgetting its intended quarry. All its efforts now were spent trying to stop the gushing blood that was not only choking off its air supply, but severing the vital nerves that governed its attempts to preserve its steadily ebbing life.

After he'd watched for a moment, Ki slowly lowered the hand in which he held the *shuriken*. He took no pleasure in what he was seeing, only a flood of thankful relief that his own life had been saved, even at the cost of his ursine adversary's.

Being a huge and tremendously strong animal, the bear did not die for what to Ki seemed a very long time. It continued to fight against the small steel *shuriken* that were still lodged in its throat, but its struggles grew weaker. Unable to breathe freely, clumsied by the loss of its principal nerve-centers, the bear grew steadily more feeble. At last its efforts stopped as the massive grizzly sagged and lurched forward, then fell in a heap and, except for an occasional involuntary twitch of its huge body, lay still as the final vestiges of life ebbed away completely.

★

Chapter 13

At the time when Ki was beginning his efforts to save himself from the attacking grizzly, Jessie and Klaus were well on their way to their widely separated objectives. Their attention was fixed on reaching their individual goals, and thoughts of danger were not paramount in the mind of either of them. From the beginning of their trip into the interior, they'd encountered such scanty evidence of human presence that they'd come to think of themselves as being virtually alone in the vastness of a virgin wilderness.

In the past ventures that Jessie and Ki had shared, there'd been many times when circumstances made their separation necessary. On such occasions it had become a habit for them to check on the progress of one another when circumstances and conditions made it possible for them to do so.

On this trip the presence of Klaus had changed their long-standing custom. Though neither Jessie nor Ki realized it, they'd both reached the same conclusion. Since beginning their trip into Alaska's interior they'd been constantly reminded that, unlike them, Klaus had not become accustomed to finding himself in a place such as they were in now. Quietly and without discussion between them, both Jessie and Ki had decided to pay extra-close attention to their European guest.

When they'd first started to fan out, in awareness of their visitor's inexperience, Jessie had sent one of her silent signals to Ki, reminding him that their visitor was in need of their continuing attention. However, from the outset of their separation, long before his encounter with the grizzly, Ki had found it almost impossible to keep track of the progress made by either Jessie or Klaus. The brush clumps and vertical, unscalable, high-standing rock outcrops frequently frustrated his efforts by cutting off his line of sight.

At the same time, Klaus, in his center position, was having an increasingly difficult time checking on the progress and positions of both Jessie and Ki. While on her way to the distant ridge, Jessie was forced to zigzag constantly in order to avoid the closely spaced trunks of the trees she soon began to encounter. On the opposite side of the big, saucerlike depression, Ki was starting to weave the circuitous track that was necessary to allow him to move between the brush clumps dotting that side of the saucer.

Belatedly, Klaus became aware that while he'd caught glimpses of Jessie with reasonable regularity, an unusually long time had passed since he'd seen Ki. Ahead of him there was one of the little knolls that rose at frequent intervals on the vast valley's floor. Klaus plodded up its sloping side and from its top began surveying the area Ki had been crossing.

There was no sign of Ki in the short-grassed open stretches between the brush clumps that dotted that portion of the round valley's floor. Turning to look in the opposite direction, Klaus quickly spotted Jessie. She had stopped on the crest of the ridge that had attracted her attention from the beginning of their entry into the huge depression.

Jessie waved at Klaus, and he returned the wave. Then he gestured toward the brush-dotted area where Ki was still nowhere to be seen and turned back to face in Jessie's direction. As he turned, Klaus spread his arms wide and began shaking his head.

Jessie had no difficulty interpreting his signals. She understood at once that he'd lost sight of Ki. Now Jessie turned her attention to the area beyond Klaus. She was reasonably sure that from the greater height she'd reached she might be able to locate Ki. She'd begun scanning the cleared areas that stretched between the big brush clumps when she noticed the agitated stirring of the one where Ki was confronting the grizzly.

Jessie concentrated her attention on the moving vegetation just in time to see the big bear's head as it reared up on its hindquarters. Ki did not come into sight until he began retreating from the thick stand of tall brush. Now, as Jessie watched the big animal moving toward him, she lifted her rifle to shoulder it. She had its butt halfway to firing position before she realized that she had no chance of getting off an accurate shot at the distance that separated her from the bear.

Letting the rifle's barrel sag in her hands, Jessie kept watching in helpless fascination. She saw the flashing of Ki's *shuriken* as the throwing blade arced toward the bear. When the glinting blade disappeared into the grizzly's mouth

157

and remained lodged there, her first thought was that Ki had missed or that the animal's fur and hide had been too thick for the blade to penetrate. When what seemed to be an eternity passed and the big bear began crumpling, Jessie at last released the sigh of relief she'd been unconsciously suppressing.

Ki's movement at that moment drew her attention to him once more. He was starting toward the area that Klaus was exploring, and Jessie realized that the three of them needed to regroup and compare notes before continuing to look for Alex's claim stakes. She looked along the ridge in search of a landmark that would serve to establish the point where her later search should begin.

In front of her a hundred yards or less along the ridge she noticed a rock formation. It not only rose higher than most above a wide granite outcrop that forced a sharp bend in the trail, but it bore a striking resemblance to the maned head of a lion. Jessie marked the formation in her memory as a point where she should start her search for Alex's claim marker when they resumed their efforts; then she turned to continue her descent.

She'd taken only a few steps on the sharply inclined downslope when she reached a narrow runnel that had been cut by the snowmelt. The little ditch still held a trickle of moisture, which flowed between banks of moist earth to end at the edge of a small, dense stand of Sitka spruce trees on the gentler slope below. Now Jessie set her course along the natural path it offered.

The downslope helped speed her progress, and as soon as she'd noticed the spruce clump she also committed its location to her memory. She began to count on it as a guide to help her when she returned to continue her search. She'd gotten almost halfway around the stand of trees when the usual silence of the uninhabited wilderness was broken by a rustling sound from the tall grass behind her.

Jessie turned just as the man who'd stepped from the cover of the spruce trees leaped forward to grab her. He had his arms around her and was crushing her to his bulky chest to immobilize her before she could bring down the muzzle of her rifle or draw the holstered Colt at her side.

"Well, now," he said, his gruff voice carrying a tone of satisfaction, "you sure saved us a heap of time, Miss Jessie Starbuck. Now that we got you, we won't have no trouble at all finding out where your pappy druv in his claim stakes, seeing as you're sure to have a map that'll show us right where to look."

Since emerging from the brush stand, Ki had maintained an almost continuous searching with his eyes, scanning the broad meadow as well as the granite ridge beyond. He grew puzzled when he failed to get a glimpse of either Jessie or Klaus after his brief encounter with the grizzly. He did not slow his progress, but kept moving in a fast-paced walk that covered the ground with almost the same speed of a trot but was not nearly as exhausting.

Reaching the point where the ground of the meadow bulged upward, Ki stopped, and as he came to a halt at the top of the bulge, he saw for the first time that it had a parallel twin a short distance away. Recognizing the high earthen humps as the forking courses of some long-dry river, Ki increased his pace and trotted down the first bank to ease the job of mounting the second. He reached its top and saw

Klaus only a short distance from him, halfway up to the top of the bank where he now stood. He turned and went to meet his companion.

"I haven't seen Jessie for quite some time," Ki told Klaus. His face carried a worried frown as he went on, "Have you been able to keep her in sight?"

"Very much with ease until a short time ago," Klaus replied. "Before, she was in my eyes most of the time. Now I have not seen her for so long that to worry I am beginning."

"We'd better separate and keep looking for her, then," Ki said. "I could see her easily while she was walking along the ridge; then I had a spot of trouble with a bear. When I'd gotten rid of the beast, I looked for her again, but couldn't see her anywhere."

"She could not very far have gone." Klaus frowned. "For only a few minutes my eyes I turned away, but when again I looked for her she had vanished."

Wordlessly now the two men turned and began moving side by side at the fastest walk they could manage while pushing through the thigh-high growth of thick grass. They wasted no breath of the cool, thin air by talking. Both of them concentrated on searching the ridge with their eyes, watching for some glimpse, even for a brief flash of movement, that would give them a clue to Jessie's whereabouts.

They reached the base of the steep rise where they'd last seen Jessie. The ledge that supported the trail she'd been following was well above their heads. Above and beyond it in both directions the wall of the low cliff showed no breaks or gaps that Jessie could have entered. There were scores of shallow fissures created by the snowmelt in the wall of dark, rock-studded soil, but none of them was wide enough to support a path and none of them showed any signs of having been used by a climber trying to reach a higher spot.

"Let's follow along the base of this cliff the trail is on," Ki suggested. "If Jessie's had an accident, we'll see signs of it from down here."

"An accident?" Klaus frowned. "You speak of a thing such as an earthslide, or the dislodging of one of those big boulders on the slope above the trail?"

"Either one's possible," Ki replied. "But even from where we're standing we can see there are so many curves in that trail up there that unless we're on it ourselves we can't be sure of seeing Jessie."

"Then a ladder of some kind we must make," Klaus suggested. "Wood is easy to work."

"Muscles are quicker," Ki reminded him. "Make a hand cradle, Klaus, and give me a boost up to that ledge. I'll lower my sash to pull up your rifle. Then you take a running jump at the side of the bluff, and I'll lean down to grab your hand to give you a boost and get you up."

Ki's suggestion worked flawlessly. Within two or three minutes Klaus stood on the trail beside him. The two men wasted no time talking but turned at once to follow the trail in search of Jessie.

Held tightly by her captor, Jessie did not waste strength in what she realized would be a futile effort to free herself. Even through the thickness of her cold-weather clothing she could feel the bulging, powerful muscles of the man who was holding her. Before she'd had time to say anything to him, a second man spoke from behind her.

"Well, your scheme turned out all right, Clack," he said.

161

"We got her, and that's what we set out to do. Now we got to get to work and tame her down so she'll do what we tell her to."

"That might not be easy as it sounds, Murch," the man called Clack replied. "Not if she's tough as her daddy was supposed to be."

"Oh, it ain't going to be all that bad," the one holding Jessie said confidently. "After you and me and Slab gets through working her over, she'll be ready to tell us where that damn claim stake is that Alex Starbuck planted."

Jessie had realized from the moment she'd been grasped by the man called Clack that the outlaws had been trailing her and Ki and Klaus. In the days when she and Ki were still battling the cartel, she'd had enough proof that the outlaw grapevine worked almost everywhere, even in such an isolated place as Alaska. She also had proof that the men who kept it alive were as merciless as they were greedy for loot.

Jessie considered making an effort to break away and run, but only a fleeting moment passed before she concluded that struggling in her present situation would be effort wasted. Then a better ruse popped into her mind. She abandoned the thought of putting up a fight at the present time and made a start on her new plan.

She gasped and rolled her eyes, loosed a gargling moan from deep in her throat as she closed her eyes and let herself go totally limp.

"Damned if the bitch ain't fainted on us!" Clack exclaimed.

"She's likely faking it!" Murch said. "A good shaking'll bring her out damn quick!"

Jessie felt the outlaw's hard-skinned hands grasp her

162

shoulders, and for a moment he shook her fiercely. Jessie had undergone much worse treatment before. She did not tighten her muscles or resist in any way; nor did she open her eyes. She remained limp and silent, resigned for the moment to enduring whatever rough treatment her captors might inflict on her.

"She ain't putting on," Murch said after he'd shaken Jessie without mercy for a moment or two. "She's out cold as a neck-wrung turkey."

"How about we get her down to camp?" Slab suggested. "The quicker she comes around and we start working to get her talking, the sooner we'll be leaving this damn iceberg country and getting back to some of that fine California sunshine."

"We might as well," Clack agreed. "Once them friends of hers figures out that she ain't just got lost, they won't be in no mind to wait very long before they start looking for her."

"We better get back to the cabin, then," Murch suggested, "and move fast, before them fellows she's with get the idea to come up here looking for her."

"It ain't far to the fork," Slab said. "And them *cheechakos* ain't apt to track us. They wouldn't likely know what to look for."

"We'll leave less trail after we get to that fork it makes down to the meadow," Murch agreed.

"Naw!" Murch objected. "Ground's too soft down there."

"He's right." Clack nodded. Then the thoughtful frown on his battered, unshaven face was replaced by a sly grin. "But I got the answer. First thing that Starbuck woman's friends are likely to do is look around for her footprints. How you reckon they'll find her if she don't leave none because we'll be taking turns carrying her?"

"That's a right smart thought, Clack," Slab agreed. "She sure can't leave no footprints if we tote her. And she ain't all that heavy."

"Let's get moving then," Clack replied. "It won't be too big of a job if we take turns. And it ain't all that far to camp. Be sure we take her rifle, too, so nobody'll be stumbling over it. It won't be hard with the three of us to work it. We won't even lose no time if we tote her back to camp and work on her till she does what we tell her to."

"Now, that's something I like," Murch said. "I'll tote her my share of the time."

"So will I," Slab nodded.

"Then let's get a move on," Murch suggested. "If we start off right away, we'll likely be to camp about the time them fellows with her figure out she ain't around here noplace."

"I'll tote her a while first, then," Clack volunteered. "Then you two can swap off and lug her the rest of the way."

Jessie remained limp while the pair bound her wrists and ankles with narrow strips of deerskin. She was careful not to tense her muscles as Slab and Murch lifted her and placed her across Clack's shoulder. Then she forced herself to relax and to move as little as possible when Clack lifted her and let her sag across one of his broad shoulders as they left the trail and started across the lush meadow at the base of the bluff.

"I'm worrying more and more about Jessie, Klaus." Ki frowned. "We should've caught up with her by this time, if she's still following this trail. We haven't been separated long enough for her to have gotten very far ahead of us."

"It was on the trail here that I saw her last," Klaus told him. "That was not long before you came to join me."

"Then you said you looked up and she'd just disappeared?"

"It was as I told you." Klaus nodded. "But I had the certainty for a minute or two that I had lost sight of her because she had only around a bend gone. It had been this way now and then after we had separated. While I was the meadow exploring after we separated I often did not see her now and then."

"And you're sure you didn't see anybody else?"

"Very sure, Ki. About such things one does not mistakes make."

"We'll stay with the trail for a while longer, then," Ki went on. "You keep to the inside of it, along the rise. I'll stay on the other edge. We'll have a better chance of finding a footprint along the edges, where the ground's softer."

"As you say, Ki," Klaus agreed. "In such things as this I have little skill."

Ki nodded. His voice thoughtful now, he went on, "If Jessie stepped off to either side somewhere along the way, she's bound to have left a footprint or scuffed up some of the soil where it's not packed too hard to hold a footprint, the way it is in the middle."

Klaus nodded his agreement, and once more they began moving slowly along the winding path.

Jessie was becoming accustomed to being carried in the fashion that she was now. She made no effort to shift into a position that would be more comfortable. She gritted her teeth and endured the pain. However, after a short painful period of being draped across Clack's brawny shoulder, her head dangling down and occasionally bumping painfully into his pistol butt, she'd learned to tense her muscles just enough to control the worst tossing of her dangling head when he stumbled or made a misstep.

Her captors talked very little while on the trail, but now and then they'd talk freely, not knowing that she could overhear their remarks. From what she'd heard, it was easy for her to realize that they had been working on their scheme since discovering she was in Alaska.

"We got the Starbuck claim sewed up for sure, once we get this dame to sign it over to us," Clack had remarked at one point. "Soon as we get her name on them transfer papers, we can start working it right out in the open. And rich as that lode of Alex Starbuck's is, we won't have a thing to worry about the rest of our lives."

"What makes you think she'll ever sign them papers, Clack?" Murch asked. "She knows by now that we got to get rid of her afterwards. She ain't likely to be all that obliging."

"She will be, by the time I get finished with her," Clack replied confidently. "Back in the States I didn't live with the Apaches three years and not learn a thing or two about making people do what they didn't want to."

As Jessie listened to the schemes of her captors, she resolved that if Ki and Klaus did not succeed in finding and freeing her, nothing the outlaws did would force her to utter a word or make a move that would enable them to carry out their plans.

Ki and Klaus stood at the edge of the trail looking down at almost vertical drop-off and the expanse of the meadow below. For the past several minutes Klaus had watched in impatient helplessness while Ki moved slowly in a series of zigzags as he tried to discover any footprints or other signs that might give them a hint to the mystery of Jessie's inexplicable disappearance.

"It's got to be the way I've worked out," Ki said at last. "Jessie didn't go beyond this point and neither did the three men who were here with her. There aren't any signs to indicate that they did anything like jumping to that meadow down there."

"But why should such a jump be made?" Klaus frowned. "Here we are still far from the coal deposit."

"There's only one answer," Ki replied. "All this mix-up of footprints were made by three men and Jessie. All the prints end here, so they didn't go back on this trail. Somewhere ahead of us there's a way to get down to the meadow."

"And Jessie?"

"They had to be carrying her."

"And you think we will be able their footprints to follow?" Klaus asked, his voice showing the strain he was feeling.

"We'll follow them," Ki replied. In spite of his effort to keep his voice level and confident, a note of strain crept into it also. "And the sooner we get started, the quicker we'll get Jessie out of the trouble she's in right now."

★

Chapter 14

"Dump the Starbuck dame over there past the woodpile," Clack ordered Murch as they entered the tumbledown little shanty.

"Hadn't I oughta tie her up first?" Murch asked.

"I don't see much reason to," Clack replied. "She wouldn't have a Chinaman's chance of getting past all three of us if she come to and made a run for the door." He turned to Slab and went on, "And you put her rifle up here with ours, where she can't get at it before we stop her. Right now my belly thinks my throat's been cut, and I aim to stow away some grub before we pay her much mind."

"Hell, all of us is hungry," Slab said. "And the woman ain't going noplace. We'll see her sure if she makes a move, so there ain't much use in tying her up."

"None I can see," Murch agreed. "Besides, I'm starved

as a bitch wolf in wintertime, and I don't guess I'm the only one."

"But the first thing I want," Clack went on, "is a real healthy swallow outa that bottle of stingo we got on the shelf back there."

Jessie forced herself to stay limp while Murch bent toward the earthen wall at the rear of the hideout to let her slide off his shoulder. She lay motionless, huddling just as she had during their hike to the cabin, when the outlaws had stopped on the trail to rest. At that time also she'd kept her eyes closed and her muscles limp. She'd given no indication that she was conscious even when the three men had gone past the point of an effort to rouse her and their attentions had become a brief gloating, fingering exploration of her body.

At that time the renegades did not have the time to prolong their pawing and fingering. They'd surrendered to the need for haste in getting Jessie away from her companions. Swearing now and then in weariness and angry frustration, they'd pushed ahead. This time Jessie realized that she could not count on escaping so easily, now that they'd reached what her cautious slit-eyed peeks at her surroundings revealed to be a typical Alaskan half-dugout.

What her captors had referred to as a cabin was hybrid, part house, part cave. Originally it had been only a shallow cavern in a high, rocky cliff. At some time in its history the refuge had been enlarged and extended by the addition of a half-room of logs. The new front part had been joined to the cavern with a heavy plastering of clay at the line where the log walls met the stony rise of the cliff's base.

Jessie's covert peeks at the interior revealed a small potbellied stove standing in front of the patched line where cave and building joined, the stovepipe extending through the clay that formed the joint. Some shelves were dimly visible in the back, and several heaps of tumbled bedding lay on the floor. A small much-battered table, a low stool and two or three chairs were scattered on the level planked floor. Oddments of clothing hung from nails that had been driven into the wooden wall behind the table. She ended her observation when Clack spoke.

"You might just as well bring the bottle out here where we can get at it easy, Murch," Clack suggested, stepping away from Jessie's recumbent form. "The woman ain't going noplace now. We'll have us a couple of swigs and maybe a bite to eat, if you two ain't in a big hurry to start on her."

"When we've rested long enough to catch our breath, it'll be all the more fun when we do get around to her," Murch remarked as he lowered the bottle and swallowed the sizeable swig of liquor he'd gulped from it. "Them two cheechakos that's with the woman won't have a chance of ever finding this place, no more than she's got a chance to get away."

"Now, that's what I like to think about," Slab said. "We can take our time and have all the fun we want, and there ain't nobody around for us to worry about."

"Nor there ain't likely to be," Clack assured him. "And after we've had our fun with her, the Starbuck dame's not going to have enough spunk left to put up a fight about signing over that big double claim to us. That'll make us all legal and proper. We won't be claim jumpers then, so there won't be no more need for us to hide out and skulk around."

"I been thinking that way, too," Murch put in. "Why, we'll be rich enough to do anything we damn well please for the rest of our lives."

Even while she was listening to the rough voices of the three men, Jessie was busy planning her escape. She had no illusions about her situation. Realizing that Ki and Klaus might have trouble finding the outlaw hideout in time to help her, she started examining the interior in quick flicks of her slitted eyes.

"I have a feeling of great unhappiness that I have been the cause of such trouble to Jessie and to you, Ki," Klaus said as they stood at the base of the cliff, gazing at the little stream they'd just waded, splashing through its ice-cold water.

"You don't have anything to apologize for, Klaus," Ki replied. "Jessie and I have been in much worse fixes. We didn't have any false ideas about the trouble we might run into."

"My father has told me of his encounters with the lawless men and the rough country here in Alaska," Klaus went on. "But that was years past, and I did not understand that since his visits it has so little changed."

"It's going to take a while for that to happen," Ki said. "Just as it's taking a little while for us to catch up with those outlaws who've captured Jessie."

"How can you be so sure she is a prisoner, Ki?" Klaus frowned. "We have seen nothing that proves what you suspect."

"You're just not used to reading trail signs, Klaus," Ki said. "Alaska's not much different from any other wild country; anybody moving around leaves signs, but you've got to look pretty close to find them."

"This I can understand," Klaus nodded. "But for what sort of these trail signs does one look?"

"If we're lucky we'll find some bootprints," Ki replied.

172

"Especially where they've stopped to rest. I'm sure those men are having to move slowly, and I'm also sure that Jessie will be doing everything she can to keep them from moving fast."

"I have seen you searching the ground" Klaus nodded. "This I understand, even if to such things I am a stranger."

"Of course, there are other signs that can help us. Places where the grass has been crushed, broken branches on bushes, a wad of chewing tobacco one of them's spit out or perhaps a cigar butt they've tossed aside. But we're wasting time standing here talking. We'd better keep moving."

They pushed on again, Ki staying a half step in the lead, where he would get the first view of the trail signs they were hoping to find. His eyes flicked from the horizon to the ground in front of them as they moved steadily forward. Suddenly Ki stopped and pointed to a small, brownish lump on the ground.

"They passed this way," he told Klaus. "That wad of chewing tobacco hasn't been there very long. There hasn't even been time for it to dry out yet."

"Then they cannot be too far ahead." Klaus nodded.

"Exactly. So when we move on we'd better watch closely and move as quietly as we can," Ki replied.

Though they moderated their speed only slightly, they scanned the landscape more carefully. It was Klaus who spotted the cabin first.

"Look, Ki!" he exclaimed. In his excitement he spoke loudly, and when Ki put a finger across his own lips, Klaus stopped, his mouth open. Then he dropped his voice and went on, "Do you see it as well? That is a shine of metal I see through the tree branches, is it not?"

173

"It certainly is," Ki agreed. "It looks to me like a stove-pipe. I missed it because I was watching the ground. I'd say we've hit pay dirt. Now, you wait here, Klaus. Get into that little clump of brush and keep your eyes on the door."

"Alone you will closer go?" Klaus asked.

Ki nodded. "Of course. We want to be absolutely sure that Jessie's inside before we make any sort of move. There might be a window on the side we can't see, or a crack between the boards that I can look through."

"I am only to watch?" Klaus frowned.

"You'd better be ready to shoot, too," Ki replied. "But if that door opens and somebody comes outside, don't let off a shot until you're sure it's one of the men and not Jessie."

"In the *scheissenverein* of my homeland, I hold high rank for rifle shooting, Ki," Klaus said. "I do not foolish mistakes as a novice firing a rifle the first time makes."

"That's good." Ki nodded. "If luck's with us, we'll have Jessie out of the hands of those men within the next few minutes."

Jessie had watched her captors covertly through her slitted eyelids. She did not like what she saw any better than she'd liked what she heard after they deposited her on the floor of the shanty. The three claim jumpers were not giving the whiskey bottle a moment's rest. After each of them had swallowed a swig, he passed the liquor to the man next to him, who wasted no time in taking a sizeable gulp.

At the rate they were tipping the whiskey bottle she realized that the time when it would be emptied drew closer with each swallow. Never one for self-deception, Jessie knew that as soon as the liquor was gone she would become the center of their unpleasant attentions. Her mental view of the prospect ahead was not an attractive one. She set her mind working harder, trying to come up with a way to escape it, but before she'd had any success Clack broke the silence that had fallen on her captors during their drinking session.

Holding up the bottle that they'd been passing so freely, Clack announced, "We got a dead soldier here now, boys. What say we figure out who'll have first go with the Starbuck dame?"

"Figure out like hell," Murch objected. "I say we deal one hand of seven-card stud. High man gets her first, low man last."

"That's a fair shake for all of us," Clack agreed. "We'll put the deck on the table faceup, and nobody touches it excepting when he draws his own card."

"And nobody gets up from the table till we've all showed our hands," Slab was quick to add. "High man gets her first, low man goes last."

"Let's do it that way, then," Clack said. Fanning out the deck of greasy, dog-eared cards facedown on the table, he turned to Slab. "We'll draw for high man; he picks the first card. You shuffle and we'll all cut; then Murch shuffles and sets the deck down faceup. We draw till we fill out our hands. High hand gets first crack at the dame, low man goes last."

"Suits me." Slab nodded.

"Me, too," Murch agreed.

Jessie had been listening to the arrangements the renegades were making to protect one another from cheating in the draw. She opened her eyes the smallest possible slit and risked looking at them as they gathered around the table.

They were paying no attention to her, for at that moment Slab was drawing a card from the fanned-out deck. He did not look at it but held it cupped in his hand. Clack and Murch pulled out their selections. At almost the same instant the three dropped their cards faceup on the table.

"Looks like you got first pick, Murch," Clack announced. "And then it's my turn. Go on and shuffle. Now we're starting, I'm sorta itchy to settle things up."

Murch began shuffling the deck of cards while both Clack and Slab watched him closely. Jessie began sidling along the wall toward the rifles. In the positions they were sitting, Slab had his back to Jessie. Murch and Clack had slantwise views of the wall, but from Murch's position he could see the entire wall to the point where Jessie had now slowed her cautious advance.

Jessie waited until all three of her captors were concentrating on Murch's hands as he riffled the deck and squared it by tapping its edges on the tabletop. Again she began sliding along the wall toward the weapons. Pressing her palms on the floor she lifted herself an inch or so at a time, the whispering made by her skirt trailing on the rough floorboards almost inaudible.

"Go on, Murch," Clack said. "Pick up that bad-luck lady and let's see what I draw. I got to admit I'm itchy to see how this game's going to play out."

Jessie was a bit more than a long reach away from the rifles and was dividing her quick glances between the weapons and the table when Murch looked up from his cards and saw her. He let his cards flutter to the tabletop as his hand started for his holstered revolver.

"That must be the place where they've taken Jessie," Ki whispered to Klaus after they'd stopped behind the shielding trunk of the largest tree they'd seen near the cabin.

"It is the only house we have seen," Klaus agreed. "But I do not understand why we hear no sounds from it and why no smoke from the stovepipe comes."

"In this part of the world, it's a warm day," Ki replied. "But the door's closed, and if we're right, they might not have started a fire yet." He paused while he studied the shanty for a moment, then went on, "There's only one way to find out if Jessie and those men are inside, Klaus."

"We must closer to the building go." Klaus nodded.

"One of us must," Ki agreed. "And I'm sure you're thinking the same thing I am, that I'm the one who should do it."

"Against this, I do not argue," Klaus replied. "You have the skill of silently moving; it is one I do not have. Go, Ki. With my rifle I will your approach guard."

Ki was already removing a *shuriken* from his belt pouch. He dropped flat and began worming his way *ninja*-style toward the little cabin.

Jessie saw Murch move and dived for the rifle nearest her. The other outlaws were frozen in place by surprise, their eyes on Murch. Jessie needed the fraction of a second; she did not know whether there was a shell in the rifle's firing chamber, and to make sure she levered the action.

By this time Clack and Slab had seen her and were reaching for their holstered revolvers as they rose to their feet. In their haste to stand, they pushed the table into Murch's thighs. His shot went wild and Jessie's lead plowed into his chest. The impact of the slug sent him tumbling backward as his trigger finger closed and the bullet from the gun's red-spurting muzzle thunked into the wall high above Jessie's head.

177

Echoes of the shots reverberating through the little shanty drowned the noise Ki made as he crashed through the door. He saw the situation at a glance. While Jessie was pumping a fresh round into the rifle's chamber, Clack had reached his feet and was bringing his revolver down to get Jessie in its sights.

Ki's *shuriken* whirled into Clack's neck, slicing through the porous bones of his upper spine to sever the soft sheath in which his nerves ran. For a moment Clack froze as the severed nerves took away his ability to control his muscles. Then he began crumpling to the floor.

For the fraction of a second, Klaus, who had followed, had been stunned by the lightninglike speed of events. Then the arduous military drilling he'd gone through in his homeland asserted itself. He realized that their only remaining antagonist was Slab, who only now was sighting with his revolver. Klaus triggered his rifle from the hip, and Slab's skull burst as the high-velocity eight-millimeter bullet went home.

In the confines of the cramped little cabin the echoing and re-echoing of the burst of gunfire died away slowly. Jessie was the first to speak. She said, "I knew you'd get here, but I wasn't sure you'd make it in time."

"You are not hurt, Jessie?" Klaus asked.

His question came just as Ki was saying the same thing, and their voices blended like an echo in the silence of the cabin.

"Not at all," Jessie assured them. "But I was very close to being until you burst in like a pair of angels coming to help me." She paused and glanced at the three sprawled bodies of her captors. "I've learned these men's names, but I don't know who they are, except that they seemed to have a lot of information about Alex's claims. I'm sure that when

178

we look around we'll find papers and perhaps maps that we can use."

"Then let Klaus and me dig graves and bury them while you search the cabin," Ki suggested. "Whatever we find will probably help us to locate Alex's claim stakes and save us a great deal of time."

"I hadn't gotten around to thinking about anything but being saved from some unpleasant experiences," Jessie said. "But it's a good idea. Let's not waste any time, though. This is one place I'll be glad to leave, and I don't think I'll ever want to come back."

"I was sorry to hear that you had some bad experiences in the outback, Miss Starbuck," Jack Dalton said.

"Yes, indeed," Martha Dalton broke in before Jessie could reply. "I hope that's what happened to you won't keep you from visiting Alaska again."

Dalton and his wife were standing beside Jessie, Ki and Klaus on the wharf at Nome, waiting for the final boarding call.

Dalton went on, "My feelings are the same as Martha's. All I can say is that I hope that you'll find the way back here and let us show you the better side of Alaska."

"At the moment, I'm not planning any future trips," Jessie said. "But you may see Klaus again, now that his family has bought the coal deposits that my father claimed. I've kept the gold claims because I have some other gold mines in the country south of here, so developing these new ones won't be any trouble, and I can devote my time to the Circle Star."

"I've heard about your big ranch," Dalton went on. "That's something I'd like to know more about."

"You're surely not planning to try ranching here in Alaska, I hope," Jessie frowned. "The climate's not suitable and there's not enough graze."

"Oh, I know that." Dalton nodded. "But for a long time now I've been thinking about the outback. Meat's scarce there, as I guess you've found out."

"I certainly have!" she replied. "There isn't enough graze there, as I just said, and—" She broke off as the steamer's whistle loosed a warning blast.

"I know that," Dalton replied. "And the time between snows is short. But I've had an idea. Meat, fresh beef, is a lot more scarce than gold in the outback. I've got an idea that I can drive a herd of cattle to the outback between snows and make more money selling them than I'd ever see from prospecting."

"Where would you get your cattle?" Jessie asked.

"I was hoping that maybe you'd have some steers I could buy," Dalton answered.

After Jessie had overcome her surprise, she asked, "How big a herd?"

"Oh, about two thousand head."

"Well, I—" Jessie began as the blast of the steamer's warning whistle sounded the last call for boarding. She waited until the noise died, then went on, "If you're foolish enough to try driving a herd of steers to the outback, I'll be foolish enough to sell them to you. For cash, of course."

"Folks up here don't know any other way to do business," he replied. "Don't be surprised when you get a letter from me. And soon as I get your answer, I'll see that you get your money on the dot, before you ship a single steer."

"I'll be waiting to hear from you," Jessie promised. "Now, if we don't get aboard, that ship's going to sail without us. And I've already been away from the Circle Star too long."

Hurrying up the gangplank to the steamer's deck, Jessie stood between Klaus and Ki while waving a final good-bye to the Daltons on the dock.

As the vessel moved slowly into the deep waters of the bay, Ki asked, "Do you think Jack Dalton will ever make a trail drive to the outback, Jessie?"

"It's hard to say," Jessie replied. "You know what our old cook at the Circle Star used to say, 'When the tumbleweeds blow, keep your back to the wind, because if you don't you're apt to get all scratched up.'"

"So your mind you will just keep open?" Klaus asked.

"I'll try to," Jessie nodded. "But I'll say this about Alaska. Cold as it is, it's one of the few places where I'd enjoy living if I should ever leave the Circle Star, because it's a place where you never know what's going to happen next."

Watch for

LONE STAR AND THE CALIFORNIA GOLD

105th novel in the exciting LONE STAR series
From JOVE

Coming in May!

A special offer for people who enjoy reading the best Westerns published today. If you enjoyed this book, subscribe now and get ...

TWO FREE WESTERNS!
A $5.90 VALUE—NO OBLIGATION

If you enjoyed this book and would like to read more of the very best Westerns being published today, you'll want to subscribe to True Value's Western Home Subscription Service. If you enjoyed the book you just read and want more of the most exciting, adventurous, action packed Westerns, subscribe now.

TWO FREE BOOKS

When you subscribe, we'll send you your first month's shipment of the newest and best 6 Westerns for you to preview. With your first shipment, two of these books will be yours as our introductory gift to you absolutely **FREE**, regardless of what you decide to do.

Special Subscriber Savings

As a True Value subscriber all regular monthly selections will be billed at the low subscriber price of just $2.45 each. That's at least a savings of $3.00 each month below the publishers price. There is never any shipping, handling or other hidden charges. What's more there is no minimum number of books you must buy, you may return any selection for full credit and you can cancel your subscription at any time. A TRUE VALUE!

Mail the coupon below

To start your subscription and receive 2 FREE WESTERNS, fill out the coupon below and mail it today. We'll send your first shipment which includes 2 FREE BOOKS as soon as we receive it.